THE FORBIDDEN FATE SERIES

TEMPTED BY TWILIGHT

THE FORBIDDEN FATE SERIES

Tempted by Twilight

NICHOLE WOLFE

This book is dedicated to:

Mrs. Romayne Grangereau,
my 10th grade English teacher

Thank you for giving me my first taste of story writing.
It and you were truly a gift.

NEWSLETTER SIGNUP

Would you like to read Charlie and Nessie's story for free? If so, sign up for my newsletter to get the full-length Forbidden Fates prequel novel, BITTEN BY DARKNESS.

If you're already signed up for my newsletter, thank you! I hope you enjoy your free e-book and stay tuned for more updates, discounts, and exclusive giveaways.

CHAPTER ONE

Autumn stared at the pointed end of a wooden paintbrush. Her eyes flickered to the dark purple veins running along her wrist. It was time.

Turning her head, a smile of minuscule proportions crossed her face as she admired her latest piece of art. Jayden had snuck in the paintbrush and berries with her poor excuse for a meal this morning. The portrait took up a solid three-square feet of wall space that had once been pristine white. Once again, she had depicted the woman that haunted her dreams for as long as she could remember. Long, flowing locks of red, ivory skin, and piercing eyes of jade with ugly streaks of tears blotching her beautiful face.

Shouts and howls along with a stampede of feet and paws passed the tiny window of her twelve-by-twelve prison, which was little more than a sturdy, wooden shed with nothing but a bear fur blanket and that too-tiny-to-fit-through window. No matter how much she starved herself to fit through it. She glared at that window. Gods, it wasn't even the full moon yet. What has them all fired up? She waited for them to pass, as they always did, as the cluster of men raced into the forest to hunt. But they didn't.

She clenched her teeth, gripping the paintbrush and hovering it over her wrist. A few quick slashes and it could all be over. After several minutes, she huffed at her own cowardice and got to her feet, padding over to the tiny window. And what she saw had her jaw dropping.

Dozens of men and wolves cluttered the spaces between the houses and buildings of Blackmoon, teeth bared and snapping, fists clenched and swinging. It was an all-out battle as she saw several men bleeding, and a few wolves trying to limp away. She watched entranced for long minutes, trying to puzzle out what had happened to cause such a fight to break out. Did it really matter? If anything, it may be just the distraction she needed.

Throwing the blanket off her, she leapt toward the door. This was it. Time to get out of this hellhole. She yanked on the doorknob, cursing when she found it locked. Nadene, her witch of a caretaker, had probably locked it after throwing her in at dusk. She added her other hand, pulling harder. Nothing. Slamming a fist, she let her head fall on the door...a little harder than she meant to. *C'mon, door. Budge.* She wouldn't get another chance like this. She had never witnessed a battle like this happen within the village. Even he (she shuddered even thinking his name) would be too preoccupied to notice her escape. She had to do it...now! *So, cooperate, you stupid thing!*

She ran across the room, taking a deep breath before sprinting toward the door, her whole body slamming into it. A giant thud echoed through the room, but the door remained completely intact. Again. Harder this time. She could feel bruises forming on her right shoulder. But she wouldn't stop. This was her chance. And she'd beat her body bloody if it meant getting out of here.

Torin Delaney enjoyed a good sparring match as much as any other warrior, but these Blackmoon bastards fought dirty. Growling as yet another Blackmoon shifted, he gripped the hilt of his short sword. *Typical Blackmoon*, he thought. They always relied on their wolf forms. The first wolf barreled down on him, baring its ugly yellow teeth at him. He clipped it on the shoulder as he dodged out of the way. It yelped. It was a risky move bringing a silver sword into battle, given that he could quite literally be killed with his own sword. He allowed himself a grin of satisfaction as the wolf snarled at him for the injury. *Shouldn't have shifted so quickly, dumbass.*

He nipped the mutt a few more times as they played a little cat and mouse. Only this mouse had a sword, and some mad skills with it, if he did say so himself. When a familiar war cry rang through the air, he glanced to his left, shaking his head and smiling. *Alaric, you arrogant son of a bitch.* His best friend carried a sword almost identical to his own, and Torin knew the man could use it. As evidenced by the several scars he had from when the prick nicked him with it during "training." Alaric slashed at one of the wolves in a smooth upward motion, grinning over at him.

"Couldn't keep away I see," he yelled to him. Despite Pop's warning, he thought. His father, the Alpha, didn't like Alaric joining battles for the simple fact that he was human, and believed that immediately gave Alaric a disadvantage. However, Torin had taught his best friend everything he knew. And what Pop didn't know wouldn't hurt him.

"Couldn't let you have all the fun," Alaric yelled back, winking as he took the wolf's legs out from under him.

Chuckling, Torin returned to the snarling dog in front of him. "If Pop sees you, the fun will be over...for both of us." The tip of his sword sank into the meat of the wolf's shoulder, drawing a high-pitched shriek from the animal as its leg gave out.

Bang. Torin paused as he was about to gut the wolf a second time. *Bang.* Looking through the small crowd of wolves and his Whitemoon brothers, he couldn't figure out who was causing the sound. *Bang.* He followed the sound to a small building near the edge of the village. *Bang.* What the? It sounded as if someone was being thrown against the door. *Bang.* Closing in on the building, he peered through the window, astonished at what he found.

The source of the loud banging was a small woman...throwing herself against the door. He watched in awe as she stumbled to the opposite side of the room and ran headlong into the door. Even through the dirty window, he could see some nasty-looking bruises forming on the right side of her body. Her right cheek was scratched open, and she had blood trickling down her arm. She was going to beat herself to a bloody pulp soon. He pounded on the glass, catching her attention, her eyes widening as she froze. "Stay there," he said through the glass. She just stared at him, unmoving. Well, she'd stopped throwing herself at the door, at least. He stepped over to the door and checked the knob. Locked. As expected. Not hearing any more banging, he proceeded to slam his boot against the door. Solid as it was, though, it took a few kicks to get it to come crashing down. He stepped over the fallen door, finding her flattened against the opposite wall, inching her way toward the corner.

Her face was an orchestra of color. Bruises, blood, and...paint? An array of colors streaked across the smooth alabaster skin; every bit as beautiful as the painting on the wall behind her. Her wide-set eyes just as bright as the woman in the painting. A self-portrait perhaps? Wild tangles of red hair haloed her face with still more paint streaked through it. Huddled in the far corner of the room, she stared at him with eyes like glimmering emeralds, biting her bottom lip, which happened to be one of the few spots on her face that were not splotched with paint. No, instead, they were pale pink, plump, and ... perfect. With his eyes locked on her face, he noticed a light dusting of freckles across her nose.

He took a step toward her, and she shrank back against the wall as if trying to will herself to disappear within the wooden panels. He raised his hands in plain sight continuing toward her. She watched him, trembling like a cornered animal. Pity and fierce determination seized him. He had to save her. Pain, pure and palpable, peered from the depths of her unblinking gaze. Terror radiated from her trembling body. What had this girl gone through to warrant such a reaction to a stranger?

"It's okay. I'm not gonna hurt you." He spoke softly trying not to scare her even worse than he obviously already had. "What's your name?"

Her eyes widened further turning into giant saucers on her slender face. Tiny shakes of her head told him she wouldn't be answering the simple question. Her eyes darted to the door as the screams and shouts from the battle that still raged grew louder. He was running out of time, he realized as he glanced out the small window. He turned back to face her, taking a breath before holding his hand out. She plastered herself against the wall, still shaking her head. "I know you're scared, but if you want out of here, it's now or never." He drilled his gaze into her, needing her to comprehend the urgency of the situation. "I'll give you to the count of five. After that, I'm gone, and I'll assume you'd rather stay here."

He started counting.

CHAPTER TWO

Oh, Gods, he was going to leave. Autumn's mind spun in turmoil. He was one of those vile creatures she had come to despise more and more over the years, but he was offering to take her away from here. Away from this sad, lonely existence where she sat in this small room and spoke to no one. Just her and her paint as she wondered when the monster of a man would visit her next. A never-ending sea of terror that she drowned in day after day. And he was offering her a lifesaver.

"Suit yourself. I'm outta here," he snapped, turning on his heel toward the door.

Her body stood and rushed over to him, falling into step beside him. He glanced over at her, and she saw his mouth curve in a tiny smile as he nodded. She gulped. Men smiling were never a good thing in her world. It usually came before they did something unspeakable. She was about to run back to the corner when he headed for the doorway, cracking the door open. He turned back to her, whispering, "Stay close to me, gorgeous."

Gorgeous? What did that mean? He held his hand out again, as if he meant for her to take it. She inched her way over to him, stepping around his arm. He quirked his brow at her before shrugging. "Suit yourself." Out the door he went, and she hurried after him.

She gasped as the sharp frigid air hit her. She'd left the blanket inside, and she didn't own a pair of shoes. The ground stung her feet as she stepped through the snow the blizzard had left a few days ago. She followed him as best she could as he weaved around buildings, trying to avoid the crowd of men engaged in battle. And then, she saw him. The monster trudged easily through the snow, and she gasped, throwing her hands over her mouth to muffle the sound. Please, don't see me. Please, don't see me. To be mauled by that monster again after being so close to escape...

Her rescuer halted a few feet in front of her as she gasped, turning back to look at her. She hadn't realized she had frozen in place, her eyes following the monster as he made a beeline around some smaller buildings in the distance. He was on the hunt for his next victim, she saw it in the hard stare of his soulless eyes. As he rounded a corner and disappeared, she let out a huge sigh of relief.

"Shit, I should have noticed how poorly you were dressed for this weather." Returning her attention to the man taking her away from the monster, she tilted her head as he stripped off his heavy coat and moved towards her. She cringed as his fingers brushed her shoulder, placing the warm garment across her shoulders. He smiled at her again, this time more fully, and, even though her heart raced at the sight, at least his smile didn't look completely maniacal. "Is that better?" he asked her. As if he cared about her comfort or something. She gave him a hesitant nod.

Why in the world would he sacrifice his own warmth for her comfort? That didn't make any sense at all.

For some reason, his eyes fell along with his smile. Hmmmm... he actually looked much nicer with a smile on his face. She never thought she'd ever say that about a man. Most of the men that had ever smiled at her had been downright creepy...or straight-up evil. "Gods, they didn't give you a pair of shoes? I always knew Blackmoon could be real dicks, but this is ridiculous." And then, without warning, he just scooped her up.

She thrashed instantly, her body trembling at the thought of being touched. "Whoa, babe. Calm down." *Yeah, fat chance.* She pummeled him, hammering her fists against his chest. *Put me down, you caveman!* After several unsteady steps, he finally set her on her feet, and she bolted. *Can't let him touch me.* When he fell into step beside her, easily keeping pace with her, she tried to run in a different direction, but everything looked the same. All tall trees, bushes, and snow. Not that she would have had a clue where she was going otherwise.

"You know, I could do this all day. But, for the sake of time...and your feet, it would be a lot easier if you let me lead. You don't have shoes, so I'm guessing you don't really have anywhere to go either."

Slowing, she glanced over at him, finding him watching her while somehow not running into anything. Finally, she stopped, hunching over and clasping her thighs as she tried to catch her breath. Being locked in that building when she wasn't cleaning clothes or weaving baskets meant she was not a runner by any means. He crouched down, gazing up at her and smirking. "Ready to let me carry you yet?" he asked, wiggling his eyebrows.

Her jaw dropped. Was he crazy? He certainly didn't look crazy...and she'd seen crazy. His eyes were soft and warm, like a crackling fire with shades of copper, green, and honey tones. The longer she stared, the more colors seemed to pop out at her from the depth of his eyes. She shook her head between gasping for air. Tiny lines appeared at the corners of those multi-colored eyes as he smiled again, chuckling. He drove a hand through his short, amber hair, lifting a shoulder. "Ah, well. I tried."

Her neck cracked as she tilted her head to the side again. This guy confused the hell out of her. What was his angle? He helps her escape. He gives her his big, warm coat. He offers to carry her. Why? What did he get out of this?

"I'd hate to see you lose a toe," he said, now removing his shoes. Seriously? What was wrong with him? She shook her head furiously at him. *Stop giving me your stuff, you weirdo!* "No, really. Here. I'll at least have socks." She shook her head again. He rolled his eyes, huffing and thrusting the pair of boots into her arms. She stumbled back, staring up at him. "Just put them on," he snapped, crossing his arms over his chest as he waited.

Another few moments of her frozen body staring at him. He jutted a finger at the boots. "Before your toes fall off, babe."

She furrowed her brows at his stupid nickname. He gave her a droll look. "Either put those damn boots on, or I'm carrying you whether you like it or not."

She sucked in a breath before narrowing her gaze on him as she pulled her snow-covered foot up to slip the boot on. Her tiny feet swam in them, but her frozen toes thanked him even if she didn't.

He nodded. "That's what I thought." He turned and began trekking through the snow. She stuck her tongue out at his back and trudged along after him.

Something was wrong with this woman. Torin didn't know what, but there had to be a reason for her touchiness. He found himself stealing glances at her as she walked beside him. His coat engulfed her lithe body, the scrap of a dress she wore hidden beneath it, and his boots flopped every time she took a step. Some very male part of him got an immense sense of satisfaction seeing his clothes consuming her tiny body. His eyes finally crept upwards...oh, shit. Busted.

Her eyes drilled into him, eyebrow quirked, lips pursed. Not uttering a word, but her face screamed, *Okay, creeper, knock it off...like now!*

He averted his gaze, looking at anything but her. The silence stretched, feeling awkward. "So," he started. "You never did tell me your name?" He risked a glance her way. She bit her bottom lip, drawing his gaze to them. She looked away, and he snatched the opportunity to study her face. Despite the marks that covered her skin, there was no denying she was attractive. Copper, mahogany, and bright auburn hair shimmered in the moonlight, reaching far past her shoulders. Ivory skin, high cheekbones that were flushed pink from the cold. Small, perky nose with tiny freckles dotting across it. Bright, round eyes framed by a mass of dusky lashes. And those lips...those were what dreams were made of.

She glanced over at him, and he snapped his head away, whistling softly. He caught her rolling her eyes. "You do have a name, don't you?" he asked.

Giving him a haughty look, she nodded. As if it was unthinkable that she wouldn't have a name. He shrugged at her. "Well, you didn't answer, so how was I supposed to know?"

She contemplated that for a moment, and then simply shrugged back. He shook his head and returned his eyes to the path in front of him. "Big talker, aren't ya," he mumbled, eliciting another roll of her eyes.

They walked for a while in silence. She seemed to be fascinated by the simplest things. She watched squirrels scurrying up trees with wide-eyed wonder.

"By the way, that painting didn't do you justice."

She snapped her head up to him, head tilted, eyebrows quirked.

He chuckled. "I mean, you're much prettier in person than in that painting."

Her cheeks reddened even more at the compliment. Pressing a hand against her chest, she shook her head.

"What? You didn't paint it?"

She nodded.

"You did paint it?"

She nodded again.

"Well, don't get me wrong. The painting is beautiful." He leaned a little towards her and she immediately leaned away. "But you're more beautiful in person."

Her cheeks flushed again as she shook her head. Apparently, she didn't like compliments.

He raised his hands. "Okay, fine. No compliments."

She let out a sigh, throwing her hands in the air and spinning on her heel. Stumbling in her hurry to get away from him, she flailed her arms. He shot an arm out and caught her, her face falling into his chest. She gazed up at him for a moment, and he smiled. "A little clumsy I see," he murmured.

Eyes wide, she flew out of his arms, pushing against his chest and swiftly landing on her backside in the snow. He chuckled and went to offer her a hand up. She scurried back, snow flying as she shook her head violently. He pulled his hand back. "Whoa, whoa, babe. Okay, okay. You can get yourself up. I get it. Calm down."

But she didn't seem to hear him, as she clamped her eyes shut and kept moving away from him, her head continually shaking. He followed her at a safe distance, not wanting to make her freak out again. Then, her eyes popped open, and she stopped. Her eyes fluttered as her head lolled. Oh, shit.

He crouched next to her, catching her head as her eyes fluttered closed. Something warm and wet coated his hand. He pulled his hand away from the back of her head enough to see it smeared in blood. Oh, double shit!

He scooped her up and started running.

CHAPTER THREE

As Torin rushed toward Whitemoon Village, he noticed her hair was streaked with blood. He cursed himself for not noticing the injury earlier despite it blending so well with her hair...and paint. She must have busted her head open when she was slamming against that damned door. Stupid woman!

He passed several villagers on his way to his father's house in the center of the village, all wearing shocked faces and exchanging hushed conversation. Whatever. The Alpha's residence was the largest of the village, towering three stories high. He climbed the steps two at a time, almost kicking the door down until his adoptive sister opened the door, an identical look of shock on her face as the other villagers.

"Torin, is everything alright?" Kayline asked, her big brown eyes wide with concern.

Torin shook his head as he pushed past her. "No time to talk." He padded up another flight of stairs and down the hallway to the bedroom. Whitemoon's only healer, Nikoli, happened to also be a Whitemoon Warrior like himself and had volunteered along with Torin to infiltrate Blackmoon. So, yeah, he'd be no help until he got back, whenever that was.

Setting the red-haired damsel on his bed, he turned to fetch some supplies, catching Kayline staring at him from his doorway. "Get me some warm rags, alcohol, and bandages," he snapped a little harsher than he meant to. Kayline jumped, but swiftly recovered and disappeared down the hallway.

While he waited for Kayline to return with the supplies, he checked the unconscious woman for further injuries. Brushing the hair from her face, he saw that the scratches on her cheek had already stopped bleeding. He moved down her face and neck, moving his coat aside and grimacing when he got a good look at the large bruises forming on her right shoulder and arm. He pressed the area to check for any dislocated joints or broken bones but snatched his hand back when she groaned loudly. Dammit, where was Nikoli?

Kayline scurried back through the door with an armful of his requested goods, dropping them at the foot of the bed. He offered a quick, "Thanks," before grabbing a rag and dipping it into the basin of water. Pushing the layers of hair out of the way, he located the source of the bleeding, a large nick on the right side of her head. He washed the blood away, breathing a sigh of relief when it wasn't as bad as it had seemed. Head injuries always bled like a bitch, but the blood flow was already easing up. He held her tight as he poured some alcohol over the wound feeling her flinch.

He bandaged her up as best he could with his limited abilities, and Kayline was nice enough to take the dirty rags and water away. His gaze returned to her badly bruised shoulder and he ran a gentle hand over it. Despite his thick coat, her skin was still quite cool. She winced a bit. His stomach fluttered, wanting to look into her eyes again. Just to reassure himself that she wasn't dead, of course.

She blinked, her gaze hazy for a moment until finally, it focused on him. He found himself smiling as the bright green orbs captured him. "Hey, gorgeous. Gave yourself quite a bump on the head, but don't worry. I saved you." He winked.

Thrashing, she tried to scurry back, slamming the back of her head against the headboard. He reached a hand out, touching the side of her head. "Easy, woman. I just patched that head of yours up."

She rolled away from him, and right off the bed. He heard a dull thud as her body fell to the floor. He sighed. Here we go again. He popped a leg up on the mattress, propping his elbow on it and resting his head in his hand. She peered up over the mattress, her eyes darting this way and that. He smirked, holding back a laugh at how silly she looked.

"If you're searching for the door, it's back there." He gestured behind him. Her gaze followed his hand before snapping back to his face. Back to the door...him...door...him. He shook his head. "If you want to leave, I won't stop you. You're not a prisoner here."

That had her focus on him, but she didn't look like she was buying it. He raised his hands. "I swear. You can leave anytime, but, really, where will you go? You'll freeze to death or Blackmoon might catch you again, and then you'll be right back where you started." He could see her mulling that tidbit over in her mind. "It's your choice, though. I'll leave you alone to think about it, okay?"

And with that, he got up and walked out of the room.

Autumn stared at the doorway that the man just disappeared through, tempted to follow him through it and disappear... where? Curse him, he had a point. Where would she go? The only family she had was long gone, a vague image in her mind that she continually materialized in paint. And the idiot man had thought she had painted herself. She had found herself tempted to break her vow of silence for the first time in three years. But no. Her voice only brought her pain and suffering. The monster had enjoyed her voice, liked hearing her begs for mercy, her pleas and screams as he violated her tiny body. It was only after she had forced herself into silence that the disgusting pig had slowly lost interest in her. If silence kept the men off her, then silent she'd remain.

Straightening up, she tapped her foot, crossing her arms over her chest as she glared at the doorway. A long hallway lay beyond it. It called to her: *freedom*, but it terrified her with the unknown. Unable to come to a decision (she'd never really been able to make any of her own beyond what she painted), she looked around the room. It was twice the size of the room she'd been forced to occupy for the last decade or so. And much cozier to say the least. She ran her fingers over the plush brown cover that spread across the large wooden bed. A fire crackled from across the room, a fur rug spread out in front of it. The mantle held several wooden carvings of woodland creatures and a large sword and shield hung on the wall above it. Some of the dresser drawers were half open, and there was an array of random items on top of it. The table next to the bed held a single oil lamp, a book, and a pile of loose coins.

It could use some more color, she thought. An image of a painting that would look perfect above the headboard crossed her mind. She shook the thought away as she neared the doorway. She should leave. She didn't belong here.

She turned, taking a last look at the room and the warmth it offered. Warmth was something she had no familiarity with, at least not since her mother. And that was a faint memory, getting dimmer every day. Her mother would have liked this room, especially the cute little carvings. She'd always loved animals, even the mice that had habituated the cells with them occasionally.

Sixteen years earlier...

Something's wrong, Autumn thought as she stared up at her mother's pale face. Her mother shivered in the damp, cold air of the cell they'd been thrown in several hours ago. Autumn rubbed her hands over the bruises that blotched her mother's arms.

"Are you cold, mommy?" she asked, and her mother smiled down at her, running her fingers over Autumn's cheek.

"No, baby, I'm fine," her mother whispered as her body shook again. Autumn wanted to ask one of the guards for a blanket or coat to wrap around her mother, but, even in her short life, she knew better than to ask. It was a dangerous gamble. Some guards took pity on them, and some...didn't, to say the least. Her mother had been punished one too many times for her own mistakes, and, given her mother's fragile state, she didn't want to risk it again.

She continued to rub her mother's arms to stop the shaking. Her mother forced her arms away as she went into a coughing fit again. It had been happening more often over the past few weeks, each time lasting longer and sounding worse. Autumn wrapped her arms around herself as she watched her mother struggle to catch her breath. When her mother's hoarse gasps wrenched the air, she clapped her hands over her ears, blocking out the sound that made her feel helpless.

Closing her eyes, she plopped on the ground and rocked in place, humming loudly. Mommy's fine. Mommy said she's fine.

Autumn didn't know her mother finally recovered until her mother knelt in front of her, pulling her arms from her ears. "I'm sorry, baby. I'm all better now."

Opening her eyes, Autumn gazed up at her mother, finding her managing a weak smile. "You always say that."

Guilt instantly clawed at her as her mother's small smile faltered for a moment. "I'm sorry, mommy." She watched as tiny wrinkles appears on her mother's forehead before she grabbed hold of Autumn and wrapped her up in her arms.

Autumn sighed, snuggling closer into the cradle of her mother's body, wanting to share her warmth. Her mother rested her cheek on the top of her head. For long moments, they sat in silence, but then, her mother's voice filled the air as she started to sing her favorite lullaby.

Bright blue sky, deep blue sea
A world of endless beauty
I promise thee, in these dark times
You will know love, sweet child of mine
So shut your eyes and just let go
Dream away your worldly woes
One day, when you wake, my dear
All you seek will be revealed

She closed her eyes, letting the song wash over her, taking her away. But there were tiny cracks in her mother's voice that hadn't been there before.

Eventually, as her mother continued to rock and sing, exhaustion overtook her, and she fell asleep with her ear pressed against her mother's chest, listening to the irregular beats of her mother's heart.

"Get up, girls," one of the guards called from the other side of the cell, waking her sometime later. "It's time," he said, glancing at her mother with a face full of pity.

Nodding, her mother brushed Autumn's hair from her face. "Time to get up, baby."

Groaning, she climbed from the warm bubble of her mother's embrace and stood up, offering a hand for her mother.

Smiling, her mother took her hand and she helped pull her up. "My sweet girl," she said, kissing her cheek. "Thank you."

The guard led them out of the cell and into the sunlight. Eyes widening at the scene before her, she clung a little tighter to her mother's side, who threw her arm around her shoulders and gave a squeeze. A crowd of mostly men stood in front of a large wooden stage shouting at each other. Mostly women and young girls stood on the stage other than two guards and a man shouting back at the crowd.

Still clinging to her mother's side, they followed the guard closer to the stage, her heart hammering harder and harder with each step. Her mother squeezed her a little tighter, and she heard her sniffle. She didn't have to look up to know her mother was crying. She had heard her cry before when she was supposed to be sleeping. But she didn't blame her. It was a sad life, raising a child alone and having men tell you what to do all day long. Life would be much better without those foul, smelly creatures.

As the guard led them up the steps of the stage, a knot formed in her stomach making her feet uncooperative. She stumbled several times, her mother catching her so she didn't fall on her face in front of the crowd. When the dozens of male faces turned in their direction, staring, snickering, and muttering amongst themselves, she completely froze. Her feet absolutely refused to take another step. She tried to step back, wanting to rush back down the steps and to the safety of the cell, but her mother held tight.

"No, baby. You have to stay here," she whispered as the man on stage began yelling.

"Next up. Two females, a mother-daughter pair. Irish descent, so possibly some Celtic genes, rare indeed."

Her mother continued to struggle to keep her on the stage when she wanted nothing to do with these people. Why couldn't they go back to the cell until this was over? The men in the crowd watched them closely, their eyes narrowing as her mother began coughing, begging her to stop. When her mother finally released her to fall to her knees in another coughing and gasping fit, she debated making a run for it. The men's voices grew louder as they talked amongst themselves. One of the men closest to the stage sneered in her mother's direction as she wheezed, and then snapped his gaze to her when she took several steps towards the stairs.

"Baby, no," her mother croaked through her cough. Guilt racked her as she glanced back at her mother as she lay on the stage reaching for her. She couldn't do it. She couldn't just leave her mother lying there...all alone.

She rushed over, placing a gentle hand on her mother's back as it shook. "I'm sorry, mommy," she whispered. Her mother managed to glance at her before she began sobbing through her gasps, tears suddenly pouring from her beautiful eyes that matched the trees during her favorite time of year.

The men began yelling, and she moved her body in front of her mother, giving the nasty creatures in the crowd a look just as nasty. What mean things they are, she thought as she pet her mother's back.

"I'll take the girl," a low, booming voice called out. Her eyes searched the crowd, quickly finding the man (more like a giant) parting the mass of men like the Red Sea. They bumped into each other to make room for him, the incessant muttering continuing. The hair on the back of her neck stood up as he approached the stage in long strides that ate up the distance in a matter of seconds. Watching her with dark eyes, his lips curved into a smile. She leaned back against her mother's body in an effort to move away from his approach.

"Sold!" the man on the stage shouted quickly.

The giant glanced away from her to look at the man on the stage and her lungs began operating again. "I'll pay half the asking price for just the girl."

The man on stage frowned. "I'm sorry, but they are to be sold together."

Crossing his massive arms over his even more massive chest, the giant huffed. "I'm not paying for a woman who is obviously sick and possibly dying. And I doubt anyone else will either. It's the girl alone, or you can keep them." There were shouts of agreement from the crowd.

The man on stage spoke to their current owner in a hushed conversation for a moment before returning to the stage. "Very well," he said, nodding at the giant.

Those two words made her heart stop. Dead still. And when the man's eyes turned back to her, his smile widening, she wished she could stay and die with her mother.

"No!" her mother screamed, somehow finding the strength to stand despite gasping for air. Yanking her behind her, her mother stood glaring up...way up...at the giant who was quickly bearing down on her. "You...can't...have...her," she managed, narrowing her eyes on him. "I know...what you...are."

The smile on the giant's face never faltered as his eyebrow quirked in amusement. "Oh, I'd love to see your sweet, sickly ass try to stop me." He chuckled at her.

She remained there, staring at him, her eyebrows furrowed until *finally she lowered her head, her shoulders slumping. Turning, her mother knelt down clutching her shoulders. "I'm so sorry, baby. I should've let you run."*

Her eyes widened as her gaze darted from her mother to the giant towered behind her. When her eyes landed on the giant's smirking face, she started shaking her head. "No, mommy," she pleaded, her head shaking faster. "No, please don't let them take me."

Tears streamed from them both as her mother wrapped her up in her arms one last time. "I love you, baby. I will always love you."

Huffing, the giant stepped forward, his boots pounding against the hollow, wooden floor of the stage. "Time to go, girl," he snapped, clutching her arm and yanking her from her mother's arms in one, quick jerk.

She screamed, pummeling her free fist against the arm that clutched her own. Kicking her feet, she refused to walk away from her mother. When he picked her up, she swiped her hand over his face, scratching his cheek open. He chuckled, and she sucked in a breath as she watched the shallow wound heal in a moment. He threw her over his shoulder where she continued kicking and pounding on his back with every ounce of strength her tiny body possessed.

"I like this one already," he said as she noticed a second pair of boots fall into step beside his enormous ones.

"Nadene will have that beaten out of her in a month," the second man said, making her pause for a moment before resuming her struggle tenfold. Gods, who are these people?!

.

"Goodness me, you are a pretty one."

Jumping what felt like twenty feet in the air, Autumn found herself back up against the bed, clutching her chest as her heart jumped into her mouth. On the other side of the doorway stood a short, curvy woman carrying a basket full of bottles. Her long, blonde hair was pulled back into a loose ponytail, and horn-rimmed glasses were perched on her smiling face.

Autumn clutched the bed cover as the woman stepped through the doorway and went to place the basket next to the hearth. "I thought you might like to wash all that muck off of you, dear," she chirped, turning toward her. Her smile faded. "Oh, my poor dear. I'm so sorry. I didn't mean to frighten you. Good grief, you'd think I'd have better manners than to just charge in here unannounced."

Autumn tiptoed toward the far side of the room, and the woman watched her, frowning. "You've been through a lot, haven't you?"

Bumping into the table, rattling the oil lamp and change, Autumn eyed the open doorway again. It was right there. Just a few steps and she'd be out of here. No more weirdos popping up in her face.

"Are you wondering where Torin went, dear?"

Not recognizing the name, Autumn glanced back at the woman, who hadn't moved from her place by the fire. She placed her hands on her hips and sighed. "Well, no wonder you're terrified. Really. He doesn't even have the decency to tell you his name. Wait until I get my hands on that son of mine."

So, now she had a name to go with the face of her rescuer. Torin. And this was his mother. Well, now she knew where he got his chattiness from. She'd gotten more conversation from these two strangers than she had over the last ten years. It was making her head spin.

"My name is Lauren," the woman said, smiling again. Torin got that from his mother, too. Always with the smiling. She should be creeped out, but she wasn't for some reason. Maybe she was losing her touch. She usually spotted the creeps miles away, but no alarm bells were sounding with these two and their incessant smiling. "And the mannerless boy who brought you here is my son, Torin."

Autumn nodded slowly, glancing out the doorway. The 'mannerless boy' certainly didn't look like a boy to her. Must be a motherly thing. She wouldn't know, having lost her own when she was still quite young. She shook that depressing thought away. He would probably return any moment, and then her chance to leave would be over.

"Don't worry, dear," Lauren chirped, drawing Autumn's attention again. She set some things down on the foot of the bed, smiling up at her. Seriously, her cheeks had to be killing her by now. "When Torin told me about you, I told him to leave you be for a while." She pressed her hands together. "So, here are some soaps and rags for you to wash off if you'd like. The shower is just inside that door there," she said, pointing at the door next to the hearth. "Feel free to take as long as you need."

Autumn lowered herself onto the bed, watching Lauren as she crossed the room and exited, pulling the door closed behind her. The moment the door snapped shut, a bolt of panic streaked through her. Once again, she was locked inside a room. She rushed over to the door. She would not be trading one prison for another. Grabbing the knob with both hands, she yanked as hard as she could, the door flying open easily and sending her falling to the floor on her ass.

Lauren turned from down the hallway, raising her eyebrows. "Ummm... are you alright, dear. Did you need something else?"

Gaping at her from the floor, Autumn just shook her head. The woman didn't seem angry that she'd just broken out of the room. Slowly getting to her feet, she closed the door...and opened it again. Close. Open. Close. Open. It...it wasn't locked?

She snapped her gaze up, finding Lauren shaking her head and frowning. "You poor dear. That door won't be locked unless you lock it yourself." One last look of pity and she turned and proceeded down the stairs.

She stared after Lauren for a few moments before shaking herself and closing the door. Not locked. She wasn't locked in. She could leave anytime. Anytime she wanted. She took a step away from the door. And another. Dammit. She opened the door again. Easy peasy. No resistance. Still not locked. She closed the door again, turning away and going to examine the items Lauren left on the bed. *That door won't be locked unless you lock it yourself.* This felt weird. Whatever this was. She was not used to it.

Y ou did what?!"

Torin clenched his teeth. He didn't think Pop would take the news of his rescue too great. "They had her locked in a tiny room with nothing but a hard floor to sleep—"

"That isn't the point!" his father boomed. Pacing the length of the large study, Talon shoved a hand through his short, brown waves.

Torin crossed his arms over his chest. "Oh, really. Then, what is the point?"

Talon narrowed his gaze on him. "Don't you realize what you've done?" The Alpha didn't give him a chance to respond. "You could have brought war down on us."

Throwing his hands in the air, Torin stepped toward his father. "Oh, like invading their territory wasn't enough for that?"

"That was simple retaliation for their kidnapping of Charlie," Talon argued.

Torin shook his head. "You and I both know that Charlie, being a bloodsucker, isn't protected under Pack Law."

The vein at Talon's temple ticked. "All mates of pack members are protected——"

"And Blackmoon would just argue that they didn't realize he was a mate. He doesn't bear the mate mark. Until he does, he's technically fair game."

"He bears a vampire's mate mark," Talon growled under his breath before resuming his pacing. He mumbled something about Nessie's poor choice in mates. It was an unprecedented match, but then his newly discovered half-sister wasn't exactly precedented. For one thing, female werewolves were a rare breed to begin with. A pack could go decades, if not longer, before one was born. Add on top of that, the woman had somehow managed to make the transition into vampirism, something werewolves were supposed to be immune to. Talon had chalked it up to her human ancestry on her mother's side. Torin just wanted the two of them to pack up their shit and get on with wherever they were headed. Bloodsuckers, family or not, didn't mix well with their kind. It was already making the village uneasy.

"You've got to take the girl back," Talon said on a sigh.

Torin whipped his head around. "The hell I am!"

His father straightened to his full 6'4" height, towering over him. "Boy, you will watch your tone."

Torin glared at his father but bowed his head. He hated when his father called him that. He was a grown man, for gods' sakes.

"In the eyes of Pack Law, you have committed thievery, and by right, they can demand restitution."

Torin shrugged. "I'm willing to give up some furs or meat or whatever."

"They'll demand a female in return for the one you stole."

Well, that created a dilemma. "We don't condone the use of slaves."

"No shit," Talon snapped. "I was the one that banned slavery in the first place. This is why you must return the girl. We won't be able to meet their demands for restitution, and if we don't, they have right to declare war on us. We are one of the few packs that do not use slaves to offset the gender imbalance. Blackmoon may gain supporters among the other packs."

Torin ticked his jaw as he contemplated his options. It sickened him to even think of taking the female back to that hellish excuse of a room. Images plagued him, the bruises, the bleeding, the gut-wrenching fear that radiated from her gorgeous green eyes. Something beyond neglect had happened to that woman. It radiated from her every time he neared her. And his father expected him to throw her back into the burning pit.

He threw a glare his father's way before turning on his heel.

"You have a week to decide, son." If Blackmoon gave them that long.

Slamming the door on his father's words, he made a beeline for the kitchen.

"Give her time to sort through everything," his mother had told him. Having spent many hours of his childhood helping his mother cook, he decided to spend his time making the mystery woman some food. Her frail body looked like it needed it.

"Hey, bro!"

Torin turned and groaned. Nessie pranced into the kitchen, her brown hair tangled, lips red and swollen, and a not-so-discreet bite mark peeking from beneath the collar of her over-sized sweater. Plus, she was way too chipper considering she was normally a downright bitch towards him. Guess Charlie knew how to put her in a good mood, then. *Gag.*

"Want some help?" she asked, smiling at him for probably the first time...ever.

He glanced down at her, eyebrows raised, before returning to his cutting board. "No, thanks."

"Well, hey," she continued, not taking the hint. She leaned her elbows on the counter and looked around his shoulder at him. "I wanted to thank you for helping me get Charlie back. Really, it means a lot to me."

Glad I could get your fangy boy toy back, sis. "I always enjoy a good fight," he said, shrugging.

She nodded. "Right," she said, leaning towards him. "Well, thanks. You're the best, bro!" She gave him a quick hug and ran off before he could even throw her off. He stared at the hallway she just disappeared down. What the hell was this? She'd known him less than a week, had literally thrown him twenty feet in the air, and now she was calling him bro and hugging him? He shook his head. Women were such confusing creatures.

He continued with his cooking. Kayline came in a little while after Nessie had left to offer help, which he accepted. He needed the distraction. His thoughts kept wandering to the woman currently occupying his bedroom.

Kayline chatted next to him as he stirred the pot and she started piling dishes into a basin. He half-listened, smiling and nodding in the small pauses when she decided to breathe. After dishing out two generous bowls, he made his way back up the stairs, the tray full of food rattling, the aroma of his delicious dish making his stomach growl.

As he neared his bedroom door, he paused. Giving the frantic nature he'd left her in, he didn't want to alarm her. He balanced the tray in one hand, knocking lightly on the door with the other.

He heard shuffling inside, and then the door cracked open and one of those mesmerizing emeralds peeked through.

He smiled, holding the tray up. "Hey, gorgeous. Thought you might be hungry."

She glanced at the tray of food, hesitating for a few moments, as if she wasn't going to let him into his own room. Then, slowly, she opened the door, and every male instinct he possessed shot to attention. Wrapped in nothing but a towel, her hair smooth and damp, hanging down to her hips, where the subtle womanly curves drew his eyes. The paint and blood had been washed clean, revealing smooth, ivory skin dotted with freckles. The scar that ran over her left cheek made him want to slash her abuser to tiny ribbons for daring to mar such perfection. He snapped his gaze back up, seeing her wide-eyed expression. He knew she didn't appreciate his compliments or roaming eyes.

"Sorry," he mumbled, stepping through the doorway. "Didn't Mum bring you any clothes?"

He glanced back, trying to keep his eyes from drinking up all that beautiful bare skin. She shook her head, biting her lip as she clutched the towel closer to her. His stomach clenched and he turned away, setting the tray on the bedside table. Clearing his suddenly dry throat, he walked over to his drawers, pulling out one of his tunics and a sash.

He held it out for her, and she quirked a brow at him. Really, she was gonna play this game with him again? Fine by him. "If you'd rather stay in your towel while we eat, I won't object," he said, smirking.

She gaped at him for a moment before snatching the clothes from his hands. Chuckling, he headed back toward the door. "I'll wait outside while you dress."

Autumn's skin was still flushed from Torin's gaze as he shut the door. Her body had seized up the moment his eyes veered from her face. She knew what a man's appreciative gaze looked like, and Torin had definitely been appreciating. This time her skin hadn't crawled, though. Instead, she'd felt unusually warm. When he didn't immediately try to paw at her like all the others, and had apologized, the iron grip of fear had loosened. Torin didn't act like any of the men she had ever known. And he didn't make her want to vomit every time she looked at him, either.

After pulling his shirt, which fell to mid-thigh and hung off one shoulder, over her head, she grabbed the thick rope he'd also provided. She had to wrap it around her waist twice before tying it. Sighing, she looked at her own scrap of a dress on the floor. It was stained with layers of paint and blood, sweat and other bodily fluids she didn't want to think about, or she would definitely lose her appetite. She picked it up off the floor, tearing it down the middle and throwing the remains into the flames.

As she watched the thin fabric burn away to nothing, she breathed a little easier. She padded over to the door, her steps already feeling a little lighter. Opening the door, she beckoned Torin inside.

His mouth fell open, then he shook his head and followed her into the room. "I should give my clothes to you more often if it's going to make you smile like that."

She felt her cheeks heat. She hadn't known she'd been smiling at all.

"Really. You should do it more often. It looks good on you."

Gosh, he could stop now. Her face felt like it was on fire. He chuckled, grabbing the tray from the table and setting it on the rug in front of the fireplace. He sat down on the rug, gazing up at her for a moment before patting the spot beside him.

She rolled her eyes, sinking down on the opposite side of the tray. Whatever was in the bowl smelled delicious, and she had the urge to ask him if he'd cooked the meal, but...she couldn't. So, instead, she smiled at him, at least she thought she did. The sensation felt odd, having not smiled much in her life.

He smiled back, his hazel eyes sparkling in the firelight, which had her stomach doing flips while it growled. "I hope you like it. I wasn't sure what to make you."

That had her heart joining in on the wild flipping. What the hell was wrong with her? He was a man. Just like all the others. Only...he didn't act like the others at all. He hadn't hurt her, despite having had several chances to do so if he wished. He hadn't even touched her other than to try to help her. Instead, he'd offered her warmth, shelter, food, even cared for her bleeding head.

She shook herself, taking a small bite of the food he'd so graciously made her. *Oh. My. Gods.* He must be a cooking god because it was the best thing she'd ever tasted.

He cleared his throat, making her pop her eyes open. Oh, gods. Had she just moaned? Well, it was super yummy.

"I take it you like it, then?"

Her cheeks heated again. He had a talent for making her blush it seemed. She nodded, taking another bite, which was every bit as delicious as the first.

He chuckled and started in on his own bowl of deliciousness. They sat in comfortable silence as they ate, and she caught him stealing glances at her every so often. And for the first time in a long time, she felt completely content. Her stomach was full, her body warm from the heat of the fire. And, without even realizing it, she had drifted off to sleep...in the presence of a man.

When she awoke, she was huddled beneath the thick cover that had been on the bed. The fire had dimmed to a quiet crackle of a few flames. On the bed lay a suede dress in a deep purple color. Autumn picked it up, finding the material heavy. Torin must have fetched her this while she had been sleeping. She reluctantly shrugged out of his shirt, swapping it for the dress instead. It fit better than Torin's shirt had. She turned toward the door, gasping when she saw a pair of moccasins set neatly by the door. They had obviously been brought for her as they were way too tiny to fit Torin. She wanted to cry as she pulled on the snug boots, wiggling her toes in the fur lining. Her first pair of shoes.

Practically prancing out the door, she went in search of something to do. And when a young girl tripped up the last stair, the pile of perfectly folded clothes scattering across the floor, Autumn immediately went to help. Laundry was something she knew how to do, and clumsiness was something she could relate to.

The girl smiled when she spotted her picking up the clothes. "Thanks," she muttered. "But you don't have to do that."

Autumn shrugged and added a few more items to her pile. She followed the girl into a large room on the opposite end of the hallway from Torin's room. The bedspread was embroidered with bouquets as well as the pillows. A vase full of flowers sat on the bedside table next to an oil lamp. A garland of flowers was strung across the mantle, which held more figurines, this time of birds. The dresser had been engraved with beautiful lilies that made her fingers itch for a paintbrush. After dumping her pile of clothes on the bed, she got started folding a few shirts.

"Really. You don't have to do this," the girl insisted. "Torin would want you to rest." Autumn glanced up, feeling her face flush. "He was very worried about you."

Heat crept up her neck, her stomach fluttering as images of Torin fussing over her unconscious body flooded her mind. She wasn't used to anyone worrying about her, not since her mother, at least. It was nice to know someone cared. Even if it was a man. Oh, well. Beggars couldn't be choosers.

She waved off the girl's worries, getting back to folding. The girl smiled as she began folding as well. "Well, it's nice to see your injury wasn't as bad as it looked. When did you and Torin meet?"

Autumn had no idea how to answer that question. They had only met...yesterday? It felt much longer. The girl expected an answer. One that involved actual words coming out of her mouth, but Autumn still couldn't bring herself to use her perfectly functioning voice box. Biting her lip, Autumn just shook her head.

The girl tilted her head before shrugging. "Ah, well. None of my business, really. I'm too nosy for my own good, I guess. My name's Kayline, by the way. I just realized I hadn't introduced myself. And you're being so kind helping me with my chores." The girl —Kayline— smiled graciously, and Autumn nodded.

Soon, Kayline was chatting up a storm, telling Autumn all about growing up with the Delaney's, who had apparently taken her in as a young girl, and raised her alongside their only son, Torin. Her face lit up as she spoke of the kind family who saved her from starvation after her own parents had perished.

"Do you mind helping me take these towels into the washroom?" Kayline asked as she grabbed a stack of towels. Autumn nodded and grabbed the other stack, following her into the connecting room.

Torin's voice floated in through the cracked doorway as footsteps pattered up the stairs. "I don't know, Mum. She's the strangest woman I've ever met. Half the time I don't know what to do when I'm around her. And she won't even talk to me. Not a word. I don't even know her name."

"You like her, don't you?"

"Mum."

"Oh, don't deny it. I'm your mother. I can tell these things. You are calling her strange, but really you find her...intriguing. Mysterious. I've even heard you call her gorgeous."

"Have you been eavesdropping on me, you nosy woman?" Autumn was expecting him to be angry with his mother, but instead he sounded amused.

Kayline smiled next to her, finding their own sneaky eavesdropping quite amusing herself. She held her finger up to her mouth. Autumn nodded, her stomach doing cartwheels as she peeked through the crack.

Lauren shrugged, smiling from ear to ear.

"Well, it doesn't really matter if I like her or not. She obviously isn't comfortable around me. Every time I get anywhere near her, she freezes up and gets this terrified look on her face. Like I'm going to yell at her or hurt her or something."

Lauren's smile faded as she grabbed her son's hand. "You're gonna have to be patient with her, dear. The poor girl has been through a lot."

"I'm trying. When I first saw her, it felt like a light turned on, blinking 'save her, save her' over and over again. But now that I have her here, I'm not sure if I did the right thing—"

"Trust me, you did the right thing."

"But how do you know I did the right thing?"

"Because I know what that girl has been through."

"How?"

"Because...I was a slave in Blackmoon."

CHAPTER FIVE

Torin's mouth fell open as his heart sank to his stomach. "Wha...what? You were...were a slave? In—"

"Blackmoon, yes. You heard me correctly." His mother said, her hands twisting into knots in front of her.

"Why didn't you tell me before?"

She took a deep breath. "I didn't want to talk about it. It was the most painful part of my life and talking about it is hard. But...you need to understand what that girl is going through."

Torin's chest clenched as he saw his mother struggle to get her composure. She was the strongest woman he knew, so he knew whatever she was about to say was worse than bad. He took his mother's hand and squeezed it.

She gave him a weak smile and nodded. "I was born into the pack. My mother was a slave. My father," she paused as her voice cracked, "was a lycan, one of the pack's warriors that were close to the Alpha. My mother wouldn't tell me which one. Perhaps it's because she didn't know herself.

"As a child, my mother kept me close by and, during the day, I helped her with her work. Laundry, dishes, sewing, that sort of thing. But oftentimes, at night, my mother would send me to the older women's tent. I found out why when I got older." Tears glistened in her big, brown eyes, making him step forward to pull her into a tight hug.

She held up her hand, stopping him. "No, no. You need to hear this. You need to understand why this girl deserves all the space and time she needs."

She cleared her throat. "Lycans have mated with human women from the beginning. The females of your kind are too few, so packs have no choice but to use human women if they don't want to completely die out. Many packs do not require the consent of the slave for such a mating. And that was the case of my mother and myself. It was probably the case of that poor girl in your room, too."

Fists clenching, he ground his molars to stop himself from cursing in front of his mother. *Bastards. All of them.* Blackmoon needed to be wiped off the face of the earth. And he was going to be the eraser.

"That was my life until the old Alpha traded one of Whitemoon's younger slaves for me after I turned eighteen."

"But Whitemoon doesn't use slaves." Torin had just had this discussion with his father.

"This was before your father became Alpha. The Alpha before him was nothing like your father. He was ruthless. Owning slaves was common practice, and he had no qualms about it. He wanted a female at their reproductive peak, so the Alpha agreed to trade a child for me. I was mated to him until his death."

Torin could hear the leaves rustling outside as his mother stopped to compose herself. He couldn't believe it. His mother had been mated to someone before his father. He glanced down at his mother's arm, where the marks of her mating stood out plain as day. At least to him. Only males of his kind could see them, and they were meant to warn other males away. Were these marks left from the old Alpha?"

His mother must've seen him looking at her marks because she shook her head and continued. "Later, the Alpha heard that Blackmoon had a female that survived past the first year. Whitemoon hadn't had a lycana in the pack in decades, centuries even. When the Alpha demanded a round-up of female wolves to be used for mating, your father eventually stepped in. When Talon killed the old Alpha, his marks faded away with his last breath. These marks are your father's from the night we conceived you."

"Whoa, whoa. Wait a minute. The old Alpha wanted the males to...to mate with wolves? Real wolves?"

"Well, that is how the first lycana was born, or so the legend says. Males have far less control during the full moon, especially if they're unmated."

Good gods, that Alpha had a few too many screws loose. Mate with an animal? Good thing Pop had taken care of him, or he might have taken the crazy old Alpha out himself. And then he'd be stuck being Alpha himself. No, thanks.

"Well, really, Torin. Most young males won't even be able to tell the difference between a female wolf and a lycana in wolf form."

He was dying to ask his mother what exactly had been done to her...and the nameless woman in his bedroom. Details he'd probably cringe at (or run off in search of something to kill), but he needed to know.

"Who did it? What were their names?" He sounded harsher than he'd intended, his anger leaking into his words.

His mother's lip quivered as she shook her head. "I know their faces, but not their names. I'd be surprised if they'd recognize me now. I was just a body to be filled up to them. A carrying case for their offspring." She grabbed a spare hanky out of her bedside table and dabbed her eyes. "I was one of the lucky ones though. I only conceived once when I was sixteen, and I miscarried before anyone realized I was pregnant."

"Oh, gods. What if she has a child back there?"

His mother thought for a moment. "Well, if she did, the child would have been with her. If it was human, that is. If she had given birth to a lycan, one of the males would have claimed her and the child, so she wouldn't have been alone in that shack." She blew her nose as her tears began drying.

Crash. He snapped his head around, his neck cracking as he stared at the door leading into the washroom. He crept over to it, signaling his mother to stay put.

"Miss? Miss?" he heard Kayline whispering from inside. "Are you alright, miss?"

Pushing the door open, he sucked in a breath as he saw Kayline hunched over his? mystery woman. She was curled into a tight ball on the floor, rocking with her head jammed between her knees and her hands clutching her ears.

Kayline looked up at him, her brows furrowed in confusion. "She just...collapsed. I don't know what happened."

"I think I do." His mother stepped up beside him. So much for staying put. Tip-toeing around him, she signaled Kayline out of the small room, taking her place beside the mystery woman.

"It's Lauren, dear. Can you hear me?" His mother spoke so softly. "Nothing is going to hurt you here. I promise." She glanced up at him. "I wish I knew what to call her. It might help."

Torin shrugged. He would give just about anything to know her name, but what could he do? The woman wouldn't speak to him...or anyone it seemed.

"Dear," his mother resumed. "You're safe here."

The woman just kept rocking and...was she muttering to herself. "Don't hurt me. Don't hurt me."

"No one's going to hurt you," he said, taking a step into the washroom.

The rocking got faster, and her hands clamped down harder over her ears. "Don't hurt me. Don't hurt me," she muttered a little louder.

His mother held a hand up to stop him, shaking her head. She motioned him out of the room. "Stay out here while I try to calm her down."

"But..." He wanted to help her. Something was still screaming *save her, save her* in his mind.

"Torin," his mother snapped, getting his attention. "She is probably having a flashback episode right now. Hearing me talk about the same kind of abuse she's endured much more recently probably triggered it. Had I known she was in there..." her mother gave Kayline a nasty look, and Kayline lowered her head.

"Maybe I can help," he said.

"No. You need to understand that she has been abused, most likely her entire life, by men. If she is having a flashback of her abuse, the last thing she needs to see when she rejoins reality is a man hovering over her."

And that got his ass backing out of the room in a second.

CHAPTER SIX

Autumn could see him. Standing over her with a sneer on his face as he stripped out of his clothes. *He's not here. He's not here.*

"Let's see if I can make you scream today."

Oh, gods. Don't hurt me. Don't hurt me. He was stepping toward her. Giant steps that reached her far too quickly. Who was she kidding? When did he not hurt her? But she wouldn't scream. She refused to give him the satisfaction.

He didn't bother to give her the dignity of removing her own clothes, ripping the thin material from her body in one firm yank. She didn't bother covering herself up. There was no point.

And then he was on top of her, shoving inside her. This was good. He was in a hurry today, which meant this would go quickly. She bit her lip to keep herself from screaming as he ripped her open once again. *No. No screaming!* He liked that.

That would make him stay longer. Silence. Silence was the only thing that saved her from hours upon hours of torture.

"Come back to us, dear." A woman? "Whoever hurt you is not here now. You are safe." Her voice was soft and warm like honeyed tea on a sore throat, taking all the pain away. "You are safe here." She clung to that voice as it made the monster fade into the background, his image becoming dimmer and dimmer with every sweet word.

Lifting her head, she blinked, a blonde woman standing over her. Her blue eyes crinkling behind her large glasses. "There we go. That's better, huh?"

Looking up from her arms, Autumn glanced around the small room, recalling the towels she'd brought in and set on the shelf next to her.

"Oh, dear. You've bitten your lip open. We should wash that out."

Lauren. That was the woman's name. The one who'd brought her the wash basin and all the scented soaps and lotions. In Torin's room. Torin...the man. Who had brought her delicious food to eat and watched over her as she'd slept. Had kept her warm by throwing his own blanket over her.

Lauren grabbed one of the towels she had set on the shelf, turning on the faucet of the sink. She handed the wet towel to Autumn.

"Is everything okay in there?" a man's voice called from the other room. Clutching the towel, Autumn took a sharp breath. *He's not here. He's not here.*

"Not now, Torin!" Lauren snapped.

Torin. The one who'd brought her food. *Not the monster man. Not the monster man. Calm yourself, Autumn. He's not here.*

"Sorry," Torin muttered. She heard him huff before he walked away from the doorway.

"Patience, Torin," another female voice, this one more high-pitched teased. It sounded familiar. "Mum will take good care of your woman," she said, chuckling.

"Oh, shut it, Kayline," Torin snapped. "Wait until Mum lays into you for eavesdropping!"

"Oh, those two fight like children," Lauren grumbled. "I'm so sorry, dear. You shouldn't have to listen to them bicker," she said, more loudly, leaning toward the doorway. Silence immediately fell in the other room.

Wow. The woman had...power? A slave? Or former slave? What was she now? She certainly didn't seem like a slave. Perhaps she wasn't a slave anymore.

Autumn dabbed at her lip, barely noticing the sting as she got to her feet. Lauren smiled at her. "It will get better. Every day, it will get just a little better."

Nodding, Autumn managed a tiny smile. Her head was beginning to pound from all the commotion. She had just woken up, but she already felt like she could sleep like a bear.

"Oh, I'll take that, dear," Lauren said, taking the towel and throwing it into a small wicker basket in the corner. "How are you feeling? Do you want some ice for your lip?"

Autumn shook her head and followed Lauren out of the washroom, feeling her face flush as Torin's and Kayline's gazes locked on her. She bit her lip again, wincing at the sharp sting. Torin stepped towards her, his arms stretching towards her. "Are you okay? What happened?"

Autumn stepped back, touching her fingers to her lip. *Crap.* She'd broken it open again. There was a tiny red smudge on her finger.

"Give her some space, you two. Torin, stop crowding her," Lauren snapped, waving her hands at them. Heat rose in Autumn's cheeks as she realized that both of them now knew that the monster had taken her. Her gaze flickered to Torin. He knew she was a "dirty whore", or whatever the males called the women they violated. Tears welled in her eyes as she thought how disgusting she must look to him now. To all of them.

When Torin's face scrunched angrily, the dam broke. She covered her face as the shameful tears rolled down her cheeks in rivers. Choking on a sob, she ran from the room.

"Wait," Torin said, as she ran past him, reaching for her.

Lauren grabbed his arm, pulling him back, and giving her the space she needed to escape. Bless that woman.

"I swear, if I ever get my hands on those damn Blackmoons..." Torin clenched his fists, pain streaking from his jaw from the intense pressure.

His mother gave him a reassuring smile, patting his cheek. "You're a good boy, son. But vengeance isn't what she needs right now."

Pity. He was ravenous for it. Blackmoon blood needed to spill...in buckets...at the tip of his sword. "What about you?" he asked, hopeful.

She smiled at him, her eyes crinkling. "I already got mine. I had you and I found my happiness. That's the best vengeance I could hope for." She pulled him into a tight hug.

"Well, yeah, but some Blackmoon heads on a pike couldn't hurt, right?"

"Torin," she huffed, smacking him on the shoulder, but the smirk on her face said she wouldn't mind. Score. Wait until Alaric heard of their new secret mission.

Torin took a step toward the door, ready to go track down Alaric and give him the good news, but his mother snagged his sleeve. "Wait a minute. Before you go do something foolish," she said, giving him a knowing look. Damn, the woman knew him too well. "Why don't you help Kayline finish up her chores?"

Torin's shoulders slumped. "But Mum..."

"Yeah, Tor, your girlfriend can help, why not you?" Kayline whined, poking him the shoulder.

"Kayline," Lauren said sternly even though her lips twitched with a suppressed smile.

Torin spent the next hour or so being relentlessly teased by Kayline as he helped her fold laundry, wash dishes, and something called "dry dusting" according to Kayline. Why women felt the need to wipe dust off a shelf that would only reaccumulate there the next day was beyond him. But dust he did. Anything to make Mum happy. Later, she joined them, and they all chatted happily through their chores before moseying into the kitchen to start dinner.

"I'm gonna go fetch the, um, woman. Ya know, in my, um—"

"Bedroom," Kayline finished, nudging him in the shoulder.

Torin rolled his eyes before walking away.

"Mum, when am I allowed to have a guy in my bedroom?" Kayline asked.

"Oh, Kayline," his mother sighed. "You're not old enough yet. Maybe in a few years"

"Years?! I'm almost twenty!"

His mother shrugged. "Age is just a number. You're not ready yet."

Shaking his head and chuckling to himself, Torin ascended the stairs two at a time. He really wanted to see if the woman was feeling any better. And hopefully get some kind of a name to call her.

He took a breath before knocking softly on the door. He heard a thud inside and had a sneaking suspicion that despite his soft knocking, she'd still jumped and possibly fallen off the bed. He waited a few moments before knocking again, and this time the door opened a moment later.

Her eyes were red-rimmed and slightly puffy, and her hair was in a wild tangle again.

"Hey, gorgeous," he said, putting on a charming smile. She didn't smile back. One tough nut to crack, this one. "I was wondering if you'd like to come down and help us with dinner."

She considered that for a moment and looked to be quite torn.

"Oh, come on. You can't stay cooped up in here forever. Please." He gave her his puppy dog eyes. They worked on Mum like a charm...at least they used to when he was younger.

He caught the corner of her lips curve into a small smile as she rolled her eyes and nodded, turning away to go back into the bedroom. He followed her in, seeing that she had dragged the large blanket back onto the bed, which was now hanging halfway off the bed. Yep, she'd fallen off the bed. He smiled to himself as he glanced over at her as she pulled on the moccasins Kayline had brought for her. "They're my old pair," Kayline had said as she'd shoved them into his hands. "I've outgrown them, but it looks like they might fit her tiny feet pretty well." And the way the woman smiled to herself as she tied them made him want to give that annoying little sister of his a big, fat hug.

"You like the boots, then?" he asked.

Glancing up at him, she quickly wiped the smile off her face. Damn. He'd have to start stalking her if he wanted to see her smile apparently. Luckily, stealth was one of his talents. She nodded.

"Good, I'm glad. C'mon, then. Let's go see if Kayline has burned anything yet."

Tilting her head, she gave him a baffled look. He chuckled. Watching her try to figure his family out was becoming quite entertaining. She followed him out the room and down the stairs.

"Kayline is a terrible cook," he told her as they entered the kitchen.

"Hey!" Kayline cried. "I heard that. I burned bread one time. When I was ten." She smiled at the woman. "Don't let my bratty brother fool you. He loves when I make him pizza in the summer."

The woman's gaze darted between the two of them, still looking baffled.

"Oh, you two. Always bickering. If you weren't both taller than me, I'd spank the both of you." His mother turned away from the stove. "Torin, why don't you show her around the village. The winter solstice is coming up, so the village is simply buzzing right now."

"Good idea, Mum," Torin said, about to grab the woman's hand, but she yanked it away as soon as he brushed his fingers against her skin. Oh, right. That was fine. He didn't know why he tried to hold her hand anyway. Not like she couldn't follow him on her own.

"Why does he get to show her around?"

"Kayline Elizabeth Delaney, would you stop your whining!" his mother snapped loudly. "I'm about to send you to your room until the solstice!"

The woman's eyes widened, and she shrank away from his mother, bumping into him and jumping out of the way.

"Mum," he whispered harshly, catching his mother's attention.

"Oh, I'm sorry, dear," she said, giving Kayline a harsh look. Kayline quickly turned back to the stove, becoming very occupied with stirring the large pot.

Torin led the way to the door, grabbing one of his mother's shawls that hung by the door. He wrapped it around the woman's shoulder, and she stiffened, her entire body freezing. It wasn't until he stepped away that he saw her start to breathe again.

He smiled at her, holding the door open for her. It took her a moment, but after he waved his hand toward the door, she stepped out the door.

Walking through the new village, Autumn was amazed by how many children ran around, laughing and playing in the snow. One group of little ones had all fallen into the snow and were waving their arms up and down, giggling at each other. Another group of children were piling large balls of snow on top of each other. And when a ball of snow whizzed past her face, making her jump back into Torin, she had to suppress the urge to run back into the house. Torin touched her shoulder and she flinched.

"Hey, Kalen! Watch where you're throwing those snowballs!" Torin yelled to a boy several yards away, who had just whipped another ball of snow at another boy. *Why would they do that?*

"Torin!" the boy named Kalen yelled. "Come play with us!"

"Torin's on my team!" another boy yelled.

"No, he's on mine!" a little girl yelled.

It was a game? Why would the children be playing games? Children did chores. They didn't play games.

The little girl twirled over toward them. "Hey, Torin. Who's your new friend?" she asked, smiling sweetly.

Kalen whistled. "Torin's got a girlfriend. Torin's got a girlfriend."

Autumn glanced up at Torin, who was smiling. Did he like these children calling her his girlfriend? He shouldn't.

"Well, Vicky, my friend hasn't told me her name yet. Maybe you can help me with that?" He looked down at her, a smirk smashed across his face.

The little girl, Vicky, jumped up and down. "Oh, oh, tell us your name! Tell us your name!"

Crap. She couldn't tell them anything. *Nope. Nope. Nope.* She backed away, shaking her head and waving her hands in front of her. She glared over at Torin. Stupid man. He'd gotten her into this mess.

His smirk widened. Ugh! What a jerk! He shrugged. "Well, kids. If she won't tell us her name, maybe we can come up with a nickname."

There was an abundance of agreements as several of the children started jumping around Torin, some of them trying to climb up his body. She crossed her arms over her small chest, glaring at him. A nickname. Was he serious?

He put his hands up. "Hey, if you refuse to tell me what to call you, then this is what you get. All you have to do is open that pretty mouth of yours and tell me your name. Otherwise... kids, what should we call my new friend?"

There was a chorus of suggestions.

"Snow Angel!"

"Barbie!"

"Pretty lady!"

"Red!"

"Minnie the Mute!"

Autumn rolled her eyes and quirked a brow at Torin, who was shaking with laughter. And the names continued. She stomped her foot, turning away from him. Jerk!

"Okay, okay," Torin finally called. "Settle down. Those were all great names. Really." He came up beside her, and she reluctantly looked up at him. He was still beaming. Ugh! "But I think I'll just keep calling her gorgeous for now."

She gaped at him, her brows furrowing.

"Want to tell me your name now, gorgeous?" he asked, smiling from ear to ear.

She had the urge to smack that smile off his face, but instead, gave him a nasty look and stomped away, not having a clue where she was going. Just away from him.

She heard Torin's soft footfalls scurrying through the snow behind her, and she found herself glancing back at him every few minutes. He flashed her a big grin every time and winked at her. Oh, the nerve of that guy! When she glanced back at him a final time, she found herself frowning when he didn't look at her and smile.

Oof! Stumbling backwards, Torin's arms once again wrapped around her, saving her from landing in the snow and making a clumsy fool of herself. Well, more so than she already had, at least.

"Sorry, miss. I wasn't watching where I was --- Torin?" The man she'd crashed into looked at the two of them before grinning. "Torin, my man. Who's your very pretty friend?" The man grabbed her hand and tried to bring it up to his mouth, but she snatched it back. What was with men and thinking they could paw at her all the time?! His big, fat grin faded as his blue eyes darted to Torin.

"Alaric, this is my new friend, Gorgeous. Gorgeous, meet my best friend, Alaric," Torin chirped, a wide smile stretched across his own gorgeous face, dimples appearing in his scruffy cheeks, which only added to his aura of attraction. Autumn sighed and rolled her eyes at him. *Stop calling me that!* She wanted to scream at him. And she almost opened her mouth to do so. She clenched her teeth and narrowed her gaze. Infuriating man!

Alaric raised an eyebrow. "Gorgeous, huh? Well, the name suits you.... Gorgeous." He winked at her.

Oh, good gods. These men were insufferable! Then, Torin released her, his arms slipping from her waist. She jumped from his grasp, silently cursed herself for not realizing. *You're getting too lax around this one, woman. Keep your guard up!* She frowned at the two men who couldn't keep their grubby hands off her.

"She's a jumpy one, isn't she? Bet she keeps you on your toes, buddy," Alaric said, nudging Torin's side.

Torin smiled over at her, his eyes crinkling in amusement. "She sure does."

Autumn shoved her hands onto her hips as she shot Torin a haughty look. *Stop acting as if we're a thing, you presumptuous ass!*

Alaric chuckled. "Uh oh! Trouble in paradise already? Man, you never were good with the ladies."

Torin raised an eyebrow at his friend. "Oh, really?" He swiftly shoved Alaric's shoulder, sending him tumbling into the snow. "Right back at ya...buddy."

Autumn shook her head as the two commenced a wrestling match, which turned into a snowball fight. She almost laughed out loud when Alaric managed to smash a snowball right in Torin's yelling mouth, effectually muffling him. Clutching her hand over her mouth, she tried to stifle the roar of laughter that was making her whole body shake.

CHAPTER SEVEN

Torin spat the snowball out of his mouth and crouched down as he prepared to spring up and tackle Alaric. Alaric was about to let another ball sail when a loud snort made them both pause. Torin turned his head, finding the woman in a fit of laughter. Her body shook with it, and the hand clasped over her mouth stifled the snorts of laughter but didn't silence them completely.

"You think that was funny, do you?" he asked her, gathering snow in his hands.

The snorts ceased as her eyes widened catching sight of the ball in his hand. She shook her head frantically, stumbling backwards.

"Well, personally, I think your ugly mug looked much better that way," Alaric said, slapping his knee as he gave a goofy grin.

"No one asked you," he snapped at Alaric, his gaze on the woman as he jumped towards her, making her squeal as she turned and took off. He launched the snowball, falling just short of her, but making her shriek again.

After she was out of earshot, he whispered to Alaric, "Hey, got a secret mission for us. I'll give you details later, but it involves some Blackmoon heads rolling."

He wiggled his eyebrows, and Alaric gave him a sly smile, rubbing his hands together. "Sounds like my kinda fun."

He clapped Alaric on the shoulder and winked. "I knew I could count on you, buddy."

Alaric's smile widened as he flashed some pearly whites. "Always, my brother from another mother."

Chuckling, Torin took off to catch up with her, which was easy enough. He found her huffing and puffing as she slowly ran out of steam halfway through the village. "Almost got you with that snowball," he said easily as he jogged backwards beside her, smiling at her flushed cheeks and puffs of mist as she huffed.

Halting, she grasped her thighs as she heaved in great breaths, glaring green eyes narrowing on him.

He reached his hand out, grazing her fingers. "Hey, come on. I'm sorry. I thought you could use a bit of fun."

She snatched her hand away, glaring even harder at him. He got the message: Don't touch. "You really don't like being touched, do you?"

Her gaze softened instantly, sadness dimming the fierce glare. She looked away, shaking her head.

He nodded. "I understand. I promise I won't touch you again."

Her wide eyes lifted to stare at him as shock spread across her pale face. When her brows creased together, her lips frowning for just a moment before she composed herself, his stomach did a somersault.

Out of the corner of his eye, he spotted Nessie and Charlie gliding through the snow in that all-too-graceful way bloodsuckers walked. Nessie's gaze landed on his face, and she waved. Charlie whispered something to her even his ears couldn't pick up. And then, they were walking toward them. He groaned, and the woman turned to see what he was looking at. She didn't like what she saw any more than he had. She scurried backwards, her eyes wide as she shook her head frantically. It was Nessie she was staring at before she collapsed into the snow, clutching her ears and snapping her eyes shut.

The two vampires stopped in their tracks, staring at the woman with curious faces. He stepped in front of her body, blocking her from view.

Nessie, the persistent pain in the ass, peered around him. Her hazel eyes that regrettably matched his own widened as she glanced back at him. "I know her."

He quirked his brow. "Really? How?"

"I was thrown into a room with her while I was a captive at Blackmoon."

His heart clenched, the soppy bastard. "Why were you taken captive?" She must have done something, right?

"It was before I was turned. They tried to auction me off as a slave, but the Alpha claimed me."

That son of a bitch! That pack (or at least its leader) needed to go. Just another thing to add to his secret mission agenda, then. Oh, fun. Alaric would be thrilled.

"Thankfully, Charlie showed up before anything... um... unfortunate happened."

"Did he try to...to..." Gods, he couldn't even say it!

Nessie's throat contacted as she swallowed hard. She nodded stiffly, Charlie's jaw clenching as he wrapped an arm around her.

He looked at the male, the vampire that had saved her. He glanced down at the woman curled in the snow. He wanted to comfort her the same way Charlie was comforting his sister. Charlie had saved Nessie from the fate that both his mother and this poor woman had suffered. He wished he could have saved his red-haired beauty, but he couldn't. There was, however, one thing he could do.

His gaze found Charlie's bright blue hues, narrowing. "That motherfucker needs to die," he growled.

The corner of the vampire's mouth kicked up for a moment as he nodded. "Agreed." He stuck his hand out. "You have my aid whenever it is needed, I assure you."

Torin hesitated. To work with a vampire was against everything he had ever known. They were the enemy. Period. But this vampire was his sister's mate, and he was proving far less dangerous to his family than that fucking Blackmoon Alpha. Finally, after a long moment, he grasped Charlie's hand and shook. So be it.

Torin crouched down, tempted to reach out and touch the shaking woman. His body hummed as he drew near, and it took effort to deny himself a simple caress. Touch was how his people offered comfort, but he knew as he pulled his hand back from her that she would not be comforted by his touch.

"Gods, I wish I knew your name," he murmured to her. To at least be able to speak to her and call her by her own name.

Those frightfully mesmerizing eyes peaked out over her arm, surveying him and softening for a moment before she caught sight of Nessie behind him and hid her eyes again.

He glared behind him. "Just go. You're making her worse."

Nessie's eyes dropped as she nodded, glancing down at the woman one last time before turning away. Charlie gave him a stern look before turning and following his mate.

He watched them until they disappeared around the edge of a shed. Turning back to the woman, he stretched his arm out, clenching his fist as he stopped himself just short of touching her. His instincts were proving difficult to ignore. He gazed down at her, thinking she could use a hug, and wondering if she'd ever be able to accept one from him. Or anyone for that matter. It was that bastard Alpha's fault. Yeah, he was definitely going to pay...in blood. Buckets of it.

"It's okay. They're gone now," he whispered.

The woman lifted her head, her eyes darting around before settling on his face. The intense look she gave him made his heart race. He found himself holding a hand out. Her throat moved as she started at his hand and his chest tightened painfully.

After long moments, she took a deep breath and slid her fingers over his open palm. Warmth spread through him as sparks of pleasure radiated from their joined hands. He pulled her gently to her feet, her eyes captivating him. Suddenly, the thought of kissing her flooded his mind. Without realizing, he leaned in. Her eyes widened, drawing him deeper, as her lips parted on a silent gasp. It only made him want to devour that perfect mouth of hers even more.

"Hey, lover boy, you can make out with your girlfriend later. Mum says it's time for dinner." Kayline's voice chirped as she skipped towards them. The woman slid her hand out of his and averted her gaze away. He threw a glare at Kayline, growling. She only smiled wider and beckoned them to follower her back to the house.

CHAPTER EIGHT

Autumn fidgeted in her chair that Torin had pulled back for her. He then swiftly claimed the chair next to her. She kept catching him watching her when she tried to glance at him. She didn't know why she wanted to look at him, other than he was quite nice to look at. And she was pretty sure he had wanted to kiss her...

What was he thinking? And why hadn't she run away screaming? She had removed her hand from his easily enough once Kayline had showed up, even felt a twinge of disappointment at the girl's arrival. Gods, what had *she* been thinking?

"Potatoes?"

Autumn looked up at Torin's smiling face as he held a large bowl and spoon. She nodded and he piled a mound of fluff onto her large plate. Lauren slapped a chicken leg alongside the potatoes, and Kayline followed with a gracious helping of carrots. She looked down at the mountain of food in front of her. How did they expect her to eat all of that?

Then, another man swept into the room. Her body seized up as she saw the familiar paw mark on his forehead. The mark of an Alpha. Yes, she was all too familiar with that mark. She just about fell off her chair at the sight.

Lauren gave the man a smile and handed him a plate piled with even more food than her own plate. He raised an arm and she realized both were covered in large, tribal tattoos. The same ones a handful of males had back at Blackmoon. A wave of relief swept over her. None of the males with those markings had ever come to her.

"Good evening, my love. We have a guest tonight." Lauren turned toward her and the male's hard gaze landed on her, making her want to fade into the chair. "Dear, this is my mate, Talon, Torin's father.

Talon quirked his heavy brow, his face tense and unsmiling. Serious wasn't even close to describing him. He was...pure intimidation. And it was clear this powerful male didn't like her being here.

"Don't mind my father," Torin interjected, narrowing his eyes on the male across the table. "As Alpha, he's not sure what to do with you."

"Torin," his father growled.

"What do you mean, dear?" Lauren asked, her gaze flickering over to the older male. "Talon?"

Talon shrugged. "Don't worry yourself over it. It's my business, not yours." He threw a frightening glare at Torin.

Lauren pursed her lips as she quietly returned to her meal. The remainder of the meal passed in silence, the tension making Autumn's skin prickle.

Torin stood the moment he'd scarfed his food down, his chair screeching against the floor. "Would you like to resume our walk?" he asked, looking down at her.

Autumn found herself nodding without hesitation. In such a hurry to get away from the awkward tension, not to mention she seemed to have bad luck with Alphas, she mindlessly grabbed his hand to pull herself out of her chair.

Torin glanced down at her hand before his lips curved in a barely-there smile. As she followed Torin outside, she glimpsed the two women at the table smile at each other while the male sat rigidly, scowling after her.

"Sorry about Pop," Torin said as he fell into step beside her. "He doesn't warm up to people easily."

No kidding, Autumn wanted to say and barely caught herself before the words blurted out.

An hour or so later, Autumn had been introduced to half the village it seemed. The lady that tended the milked the goats had laughed at Torin's silly nickname, making her want to kick him in the shins. The boys had teased, and the girls had giggled. By the time they made it back to Torin's house, even the chilly air couldn't account for her flushed cheeks. When Torin's fingers brushed over her shoulders as he slid her coat off her, her body stiffened. But she didn't jump away, eager to flee from him. In fact, even though he had just embarrassed the ever-living shit out of her, she wasn't in a rush to get away from him. His energy was contagious, and he seemed to always be smiling, which made her want to smile, too.

But as she glanced out the window at the setting sun, she knew the day was coming to an end. And that meant everyone retiring to bed.

She followed Torin up the stairs, mindlessly heading towards his room. Until he veered down a different hallway. He opened the door at the end of it, beckoning her inside. Quirking her brows, she stepped into the spacious room. A small bed was situated in the far corner, a deep sage colored quilt atop it. Another oil lamp stood on the bedside table and a fire crackled in the little fireplace in the opposite corner of the room, a handwoven rug that matched the bed lay in front, and a garland of pink flowers sat across the mantle.

"Mum and Kayline got the guest room all ready for you," Torin stated, a hint of a frown on his face.

Autumn glanced around the room, warm and cozy as the rest of the house, wondering what could be making him frown.

"Well, I'll leave you alone to rest, then," he muttered, dragging his feet out of the room.

Wait, what? The thought of being all alone in the strange room had her hyperventilating. What if that other male came for her in the night? He hadn't set off any creeper alarms, but she got the distinct feeling he did not want her here at all. What if he threw her out in the snow while Torin was sleeping in the other room?

She rushed after Torin, tearing straight into his room, a wave of relief settling over her as his face came into view.

Torin stared at her, both eyebrows raised. "Is something wrong with the guest room? Do you need something else?"

She nodded. His eyes did a quick sweep of her before he nodded and snapped his fingers. "Of course. Pajamas!"

What the hell were those? No! Torin grabbed something from one of his dressers, holding it out for her. She shook her head, sighing. This no-talking thing wasn't working out so great here. Then again, she'd never had so many people to talk to in her life. She opened her mouth, her frustration getting the best of her.

In a second, Torin's gaze locked onto her lips. Eyes sparkling with interest. And that had her snapping her mouth shut and all thoughts of actually utilizing her vocal chords gone.

Torin cursed as the woman snapped that pretty mouth closed without uttering a peep. He'd been so close to finally hearing her voice. He dropped his arm, shirt still clutched in his hand.

"Gods, why won't you just talk to me?" he snapped, fingers spearing through his hair. "I'm not a fucking mind reader, woman."

After taking a breath, he glanced over at her again, finding her stunning gaze wide with fear as she backed away from him, heading for the door. The fear in her eyes had his chest clenching in regret. Without thinking, he reached for her to apologize. And she bolted.

"No, wait. I'm sorry...Gorgeous? Shit!" He needed her goddamn name!

He paced his room as he tried to figure out how to handle such a clearly damaged woman. He'd barely raised his voice and she'd fled in fear. After stewing in contemplation a while longer, he decided it was best he left her alone...for now, at least. She needed time to heal, and his presence probably wasn't helping. He had a dick, after all. And after what the woman had endured, she didn't need another one of those in her life right now. And the more he was around her, the harder it was becoming to keep his fingers to himself. Because they were constantly itching for a touch, a simple glide over her skin to ease his curiosity. He shook himself. *She doesn't need another man pawing her up, you perv.*

Just as he was about to go find Kayline to ask her to lend the woman a pair of PJs, his mother came storming into his room.

"What in the gods' names did you say to that poor woman?"

"What? Nothing." Automatic response when Mum has a "you're in big trouble" tone in her voice.

"She was about to run out of the house until she realized it was past dark and she has nowhere else to go. Thank the gods *she* has some common sense about her. I can't believe you'd scare her off like that!"

He opened his mouth to ask if she was alright and apologize, but his mother hushed him up with a finger.

"Now, you listen to me, Torin Delaney." Oh, shit. Full name meant serious business. "That woman has been through more than enough. You mind your manners and make her feel welcome in my house."

She obviously didn't know of her husband's plans of throwing the woman back into that pack of dogs known as Blackmoon. But he wasn't about to open that can of nasty worms. Gods help Pop when Mum found out that dirty little secret.

"I'm trying, Mum. You know I want her to stay here. For her own safety. I was the one who brought her here in the first place. I just...I don't know how to talk to her when she won't talk at all. Nothing. I don't even know her name."

His mother sighed, then smiled as she led them over to sit on his bed. "I know patience isn't always easy, but the fact that she even touched your hand earlier is already amazing progress for her."

He nodded in agreement. The woman had been through hell, and at the hands of his own kind. It was a wonder she could even be in the same room with him and not be shaking in fear. Just having her look at him in pure terror had made his chest ache. "I'm going to give her some space. I think she needs some time away from men for now."

His mother glowed at him. "That's very mature and unselfish of you, especially when I know how much you like her." He rolled his eyes. "But...if she seeks you out..."

He didn't need her to tell him to keep his temper in check around the fragile woman. He'd learned that lesson the hard way today.

Autumn tossed the thick quilt of her, growling at the ceiling. She'd spent the last several hours tossing and turning in the perfectly comfortable bed in the "guest" room Torin had frightened her back into earlier. He'd been angry at her for not speaking. Typical male. They didn't know what to do with themselves without a woman praising them or screaming in fear. She'd been fooling herself into thinking Torin was any different.

Unfortunately, her body was itching to go back to his room. It was the familiar sheets and carvings, of course. Not the man that most likely occupied the large bed, sound asleep. Must be nice.

Well, he did save you from the monster.

Only to be a monster to me himself.

He only wanted your name. How bad could that be?

And on and on it went as she argued with her own mind, trying to convince herself she was much better off here. Alone. Unprotected. Vulnerable.

Cursing herself, she tiptoed out of the room.

CHAPTER NINE

Torin groaned as his eyes peeled open, his skin feeling uncomfortably tight. It always did when the full moon drew near. Specks of dust floated in the beams of bright sunlight that fell through the curtains, reminding him how neglectful he'd been to his room. His mother and Kayline refused to clean his bedroom. Even though they cleaned every other room in the house. What was one more? Really? But they insisted keeping his personal space clean was not their duty. Fine. Whatever. When he realized that their new guest had seen his room in such disarray, he climbed from the bed intent on tracking down the dusting rags.

But halfway to his dresser, he froze.

There, lying curled in a tight ball on the rug, was said new guest. Even in sleep, she shivered from the cold. Because the fire had gone out and the room was obviously chilled more than his body could detect. His kind had a high tolerance of the cold. If not for the human women that resided in the home, there wouldn't be much need for fireplaces at all. He promptly snatched his heavy quilt from the bed and gently laid it over her. A few moments later, she sighed, smiling as her body relaxed into its warmth. It made him want to snuggle under those covers and keep her nice and toasty with his own body heat.

He suppressed a groan at the thought of his skin pressing against hers, how soft all that paleness would be against his own tanned and weathered hands.

Whoa, buddy. She needs space, remember?

With one last longing look, he snatched a pair of leathers from the floor and fled the room. Before his imagination got the best of him.

Once in the hallway, he moseyed through the house in search of his original agenda for the morning. Dusting supplies. On his way downstairs, he caught sight of his Mum rummaging through some boxes in the storage closet. Probably where the cleaning supplies were located.

"Hey, Mum, where are the dusting rags?"

She took a nanosecond to give him a droll look before returning her attention to the boxes. "You've lived in this house for almost twenty years, and you still don't know?"

He sighed. Typical Mum response. "Well, Kay keeps moving them."

Now, she gave him a "You're full of shit" look. "They're in a bin under the kitchen sink where they have always been. Ah, here they are!" She pulled several tiny bottles of paint from the box and a can of brushes.

The sight of them gave Torin a marvelous idea.

You caved.

I know, shut up.

I can't believe you caved.

Growling under her breath, she threw the heavy quilt off her. Wait, quilt? She hadn't gone to sleep with a blanket. Because she was an idiot who forgot to bring one from the other room in her rush to get here in the middle of night.

I can't believe you caved.

Shut it!!!

Torin must have thrown it over her sometime after she'd fallen asleep. Bringing the material up to her face, she inhaled, her stomach fluttering at the fresh scent of pine and... Torin. She'd never thought she would actually enjoy the smell of a man. Ever. The monster had always reeked of...pure evil. There was no other way to describe him really. But Torin...Torin's scent was completely different.

After pulling herself away from the heavenly smell, she stood and peered at the bed, frowning when she saw it empty.

The man just yelled at you last night and you're already disappointed he's not here?

He didn't yell, he just...raised his voice a tad.

Now you're defending him!

She threw the quilt back on the bed, cursing. She was defending him. What was wrong with her?

When she heard whistling outside the door, she bolted behind the bed...for some reason. Apparently, even though she was disappointed he wasn't in the room earlier didn't mean she wasn't still terrified.

You make no sense, woman.

Tell me about it.

The door clicked open, and she ducked under the bed. Large and unmistakably male feet padded into the room, and she heard the clinking of glass as he came to an abrupt halt. Surprised she wasn't still huddled under the quilt, was he? *Oh, no, instead you're cowering under his bed.*

He set something on the bed, rustling the covers in the process. After padding over to the fireplace and depositing some twigs and a small log, he threw a match into the hearth igniting some sweet-smelling chips on the bottom. He turned back toward the bed, his feet crossing at the ankle as he leaned against the door that led to the small en-suite bathroom.

He chuckled. "First of all," he began, amusement dripping from every syllable. "I could smell you the moment I walked in here. Supernatural senses, remember? And second." He paused, stepping closer. "Your cute, little feet are sticking out from under the bed." He bent down in a flash of movement and ran his finger along the bottom of her foot, sending tingles up her leg and making her squeal. She jerked her feet under the bed, her head slamming into the bedframe, making her curse at the sharp pain in her head.

Which made him roar with laughter. What a prick.

After several minutes of him trying to get himself under control, he bent over again, his face smiling upside down at her. "Are you gonna come out anytime soon? I brought you something." His smile brightened, if that was even possible, his face practically glowing. Someone looked excited. Which put her on edge. She hated surprises. Because they always ended with her wanting to scream in agony.

Torin saw her throat move as she gulped, a flash of fear in her eyes as she reluctantly crawled out from beneath his bed. He kept the smile on his face despite the guilt and shame he was feeling. He shouldn't have lost his temper last night. He rocked on his heels. "So... I got you something."

Apprehension oozed from her every pore.

Ignoring it, he continued. "You wanna see what it is?"

She hesitated, pressing her lips together as her eyes darted around the room.

"No, no. It's hidden. You have to close your eyes."

Instead, her eyes turned into giant emeralds, and she took a clumsy step back, bumping into the bed. Whoa, she did not like that idea.

He held his hands up. "Okay, okay. You don't have to close your eyes. Way to spoil my fun, though."

She edged further away, terror turning her pale face stark white. Which made no sense. If she was so afraid of him, why had she come into his room in the middle of the night to sleep on the floor? Wouldn't she just avoid him? She had sought him out. Didn't that mean she wanted to be around him?

"C'mon. I'm sure you'll really like it," he coaxed, keeping his voice soft and soothing.

Or at least he thought he was until she ran out the room again. What. The. Fuck.

They're all crazy, sadistic bastards! Autumn thought as she once again found herself making a mad dash through the house. In less than twenty-four hours. Why did all men have to be complete perverts?

This time she didn't make it to the front door. No, this time she crashed headfirst into Kayline, dishes crashing to the floor along with both of them.

"You need your own warning sign." Kayline chuckled as she helped Autumn to her feet. Icy blue hues studied her face. Kayline frowned. "Dear gods, you look like you've seen a ghost." Sighing heavily, she shook her head. "What did that brother of mine do now?"

See, even his own sister knows he's done something unspeakable!

"Wait until Mum hears he's gone and scared the beZues out of you again..."

"Wait until Mum hears what?" Lauren snapped from behind them, making Autumn jump ten feet away clutching her chest. These people were going to give her a heart attack.

Lauren glanced at her. "Sorry, dear. Didn't mean to frighten you. What did Torin do now?"

"Spooked her again, I guess," Kayline answer, shrugging. "She was running from upstairs when we bumped into each other...well, more like collided, actually."

Lauren's face puckered in confusion. "That's odd. He was jabbering on about giving her a gift earlier."

Kayline clapped her hands. "Oh, a gift! What was it?"

Why in the world did she look so excited? Gifts were terrible!

"Torin wanted to surprise her..." Lauren whispered.

Surprises were even worse! What was wrong with them?

"Did Torin give you the gift?" Lauren asked her.

She shook her head violently, waving her hands in front of her. No way, and she didn't want it.

"Why would she be afraid of a gift, Mum?" Kayline eyed her like she was crazy.

Lauren on the other hand, had a face full of pity. "I know."

Autumn pointed at Lauren as she gave Kayline a stern look. *See, I'm not the crazy one!*

"Dear, what those other men said were 'gifts'...well, that's not what Torin is giving to you. I promise. He showed me this morning. I think you're going to love it." Lauren smiled at her, nodding her head.

Autumn stared at the woman in disbelief. This woman. Who'd been a slave like her once.

"What did those other men give her?" Kayline asked, making the blood drain from Autumn's face in mortification.

Lauren gave her daughter a hard look, which made Kayline scurry back to the kitchen, snatching up dishes as she went.

"Torin won't give you his gift until you're ready to accept it. But you won't regret accepting, trust me." Lauren gave her another gentle smile. "Whenever you're ready, dear."

Autumn nodded as the woman walked off into another room, leaving her to figure out if she could bring herself to go back to Torin's room. Because, dammit, now she wanted to know what even the former Blackmoon slave thought she would like. A gift. That she'd actually like. What a thought.

Torin ran his fingers through his hair, muttering to himself about confusing women for the tenth time. He didn't get it. He had done nothing to warrant the woman fleeing the room this time. All he'd wanted to do was give her a fucking gift!

Zeus Almighty, maybe this was all useless. Maybe she couldn't trust a man. Hell, he didn't even blame her. Maybe she could see a man as a friend. And who was he kidding. He didn't want to just be her friend. Not really. He felt it every time she was near. Every time she was within reach, his fingers itched to touch her. Just a gentle stroke. But he couldn't.

Just as he was about to snatch the gift from beneath the quilt and throw it in the trash, he spotted her. Her tiny frame hidden as she peered around the doorframe, her eyes watching him like a hawk. And something had captured her interest. Hope sparked back to life. Because that something inside him was still screaming "save her."

Inch by tortuous inch, she came out from behind the door frame, stepping into the room one tedious step at a time. But he made no move toward her, didn't even utter a word. Afraid he might scare her off again. No, he let her come at her pace as close to him as she felt comfortable. She stopped just beyond his reach, eyes still locked with his as they gazed at each other over the bed.

Silently, slowly, he pulled the box from beneath the quilt.

Her eyes fell, widening in surprise. When her head tilted to one side, he wondered if maybe she didn't recognize the gift wrapping. He had admittedly done a shoddy job of it.

He cleared his throat, holding it out for her. "Sorry about the wrap job. I've never done it before."

Her eyebrows quirked as she reached for the box, her fingertips brushing his own. He felt the contact down to his toes, and from the way her eyes flew back up to his, her pretty lips partying oh-so-perfectly, so had she.

Oh, yes, hope was in full bloom.

A moment passed as he soaked up the tension sizzling just below the surface, their eyes dancing with each other. Then, she looked down, and the moment was gone.

Despite the pang of disappointment in his chest, he tried to keep his face neutral. She turned the box over in her hand, peering at all the paper and string, glancing up at him when the contents clinked inside.

When she set the box down and gave him a weak smile, he smirked. "You're supposed to open it," he murmured, excitement blazing through him as he realized she'd never received a gift before.

Her eyebrows raised as he mouth made a little "o." Her delicate fingers unwrapped the gift without tearing a single piece of paper.

And then her face lit up like a Winter Solstice tree, her smile more beautiful than any sunrise. She cupped a bottle of blue paint in her hands as she slid her fingers over the soft bristles of the brushes. As if they were a precious gem. When she finally pulled her eyes away from her gift, they were brimming with tears.

He smiled at her. "You're so talented, I figured you needed a new set. I hope you like them."

Bam. The floodgates opened. Instinct had him rushing over to her. "No, no. Don't cry. I'm sorry...you don't have to keep them..." He snatched his hand back just before he touched her, cursing himself. He knew she didn't like to be touched.

And then her arms wrapped around him, her tear-soaked face pressing against his shoulder as she wept into it. The sensation took the breath right out of him. As he laid a gentle hand on her back, he closed his eyes, relishing in how perfect she felt in his arms. In his arms. At last.

She had cried a thousand times and a million tears. But never. Not once. Had she ever cried because she was...happy? Was this what it felt like? Her chest felt like it would burst as Torin's scent washed over her, his strong arms cocooning her.

That realization had her happy thoughts screeching to a halt. If his arms were around her, she wouldn't be able to get out. He'd overpower her and she'd be helpless.

She scurried back, his arms opening to release her. No struggle. No resistance. He just...let her go.

He smiled, gazing down at her with soft eyes. But he didn't come for her. She noticed he clenched his fists before shoving them in the pockets of his pants. He cleared his throat again. "I take it you like your gift, then?"

She blushed, wiping the tears from her face as she nodded. I guess she'd made that glaringly obvious.

His smile widened, shiny white teeth peeking out as he bit his bottom lip, drawing her gaze there. He had pale lips, smooth in contrast with the stubble on his jaw. They looked...nice. "I may have to get you more gifts in the near future..."

Her face heated further.

"You're stunning when I embarrass you." His voice lowered, his eyes piercing as they sparkled at her.

She pressed her lips together as her cheeks probably turned redder than her hair. Damn him. Rolling her eyes at his teasing, she returned her attention to the paints. Her paints. They were all hers. Her eyes started to sting. *Do not cry again, you big baby.*

He chuckled. "Well, you definitely take gifts better than compliments." She glared up at him, tempted to stick her tongue out. "Don't worry, I'll still give you plenty of both." He winked at her as he grabbed some clothes from his drawer and headed toward the door. "I'll let you enjoy your gift in peace now."

CHAPTER TEN

Torin groaned as Alaric's wooden sword smashed into this gut for the third time. Son of a bitch. That stung. Since when did Alaric get so good?

"Dude, where is your head at? I haven't whooped your ass this good since you were twelve."

"Please. You've never whooped my ass."

"Aww, is someone fantasizing about that pretty redhead?" Alaric wiggled his eyebrows and made kissy faces at him.

Torin whipped him the finger and Alaric roared with laughter.

"Seriously, man. What's going on with you two? You've been following her around like a lovesick puppy for two days. It's the first time I've seen your face since you spared me two minutes to introduce her."

That earned his best friend a second whip of the finger. Sick puppy? Puh. He hadn't seen *her* for over twenty-four hours. Not since he'd given her his gift yesterday and she had gifted him with... the most perfect embrace in the universe. Shit, this was bad. Maybe Alaric had a point. What was going on with him? He'd known the woman for three days, and yet he felt...consumed by her. There was no other way to put it. She occupied his every waking moment. No wonder Alaric was whooping his ass. And if Alaric could whoop him, no telling what another Lycan could do to him if he let himself be distracted like this.

No, he had to forget about her. He couldn't have that kind of distraction on the battlefield. Especially since his father seemed convinced Blackmoon would declare war if he didn't march the poor woman straight back into the Pack of Evil. Which he wouldn't do. Ever. Because he had vowed to save her from that pathetic excuse of an Alpha. And by gods, he refused to fail. She needed one man to not fail her in her life.

Alaric waved a hand in front of his face. "Hello? There you go again fantasizing about Little Red again."

Torin smacked his hand away. "Little Red? Seriously, Ric?"

His best friend shrugged. "What? She's little and she's red. Perfect name in my opinion."

Torin shook his head but couldn't keep himself from smiling. "You're such an asshole."

Alaric smiled wide and threw his arms out proudly. "You know it, bro."

By the time Torin dragged his bruised and beaten ass back to his house, the sun was fading behind the thick tree line. Patches of snow still dotted the village, most of it having melted in the sun. There were a few small heaps left where the children's snowmen had been only the day before.

He'd barely pushed the front door open when Little Red (damn, you, Ric) came skipping down the stairs. He gulped down a lump in his throat at the sight of her. The cream-colored dress she wore flounced around her little moccasins with every step. Her wild tangle of red waves had been tamed into a braid. Her green eyes shining just as bright as her wide smile. She was...breathtaking.

She came right up to him, grabbing his hand and pulling him up the stairs. And just like that forgetting about her was...forgotten.

He let her drag him straight up to his room, which she had swiftly stolen since her arrival. He had slept in the guest room last night. But touching her hand, feeling the ripples of pleasure it caused, made it all worth it.

She released his hand the moment they were inside, prancing over to the fireplace. He glanced around, finding opened bottles of paint scattered on his dresser alongside his carvings. Washed brushes lay on a towel on the bed to dry and her pajamas were thrown in a heap in the corner. The woman was taking over his room.

He glanced back over at her, finding her bouncing on her toes and biting her lip. His gut clenched at the sight, but he tamped it down. Then, she stepped to the side, and he gasped. On a large piece of canvas was the prettiest landscape scene he'd ever laid eyes on. Not that he'd seen many painted landscapes, but this one had to be as good as any the "cultured" bloodsuckers had in their museums. Trees of yellow, orange, and red hugged a bright blue sky. Stray leaves falling to piles where miniscule children jumped among them.

"It's amazing," he breathed, looking down at her beaming face. "You're amazing."

Her freckles faded as her cheeks turned pink. When she pointed at the paining and then herself, he smirked. "Yes, I know you painted it."

She sighed, shaking her head, and then repeated the motion. When he just smiled, she did it a third time.

He furrowed his brows. "You're trying to tell me something, aren't you?"

She nodded and repeated the motion again. Something about her and the painting. Beyond they're both amazing, obviously. He studied both, trying to understand. Maybe she wanted a more detailed observation.

It's a beautiful scene," he said. "Autumn just so happens to be my favorite season."

She jumped, excitement lighting up her face. Nodding frantically, she pointed at herself again.

"Oh, it's your favorite too?"

Disappointment. She shook her head, slamming her hand against her chest. He must have been on the right track for her to get so excited. Maybe the season was the key.

You..." She pointed at the painting. "Season..."

She waved him on.

"The season is...autumn."

Excitement again. "Autumn..."

She placed her hand on her chest.

"You..."

Frantic nodding again.

"You are..."

She pointed at the painting again.

"Autumn."

She jumped up, clapping her hands.

"You are autumn."

Mega-watt smile. A light bulb finally went off.

"Your name is...Autumn," he breathed. Autumn. Without thinking, he cupped her face in his palms. And by gods, she let him, gazing up at him with those dazzling green eyes. "Autumn," he murmured.

She sighed, smiling up at him, and he almost leaned down to kiss her. The moment seemed to call for it, but he stopped himself, fearing she wasn't ready. Besides, if he kissed her now, there would be no forgetting her after that.

Her name on his lips sent shivers down her spine. For some reason, his voice didn't morph her name into something ugly and terrifying. He made it sound like it hadn't existed before this moment. Like it was the first time she'd heard it correctly.

He glanced at the painting and back to her. "It's perfect."

She smiled wider. Her cheeks were going to kill her later. They hadn't gotten this kind of workout in... forever.

"Much better than Little Red, that's for sure." She quirked a brow at him, but he shook his head. "Nevermind."

He dropped his hands, taking a step back. "You spent all this time painting this?"

She nodded, wondering why he sounded so surprised. Paintings didn't come out of thin air. They took time. A lot of it.

"Just so I would know your name?"

Tilting her head, she stared at him. A moment ago, he had seemed so pleased, now he seemed confused. Like he didn't understand how important it was.

After she nodded again, he turned his attention to the painting. He studied it for what felt like a lifetime. Was there something wrong. Maybe he didn't like it.

"I can't believe you did all this for me," he mused, his eyes shimmering at her. "I'm glad you wanted me to know your name." He leaned down, bringing his lips close to her ear. "Because I've been dying to say it for days."

Good, she thought as she sighed to herself, his breath against her skin sending shivers down her body. Because her name had never sounded so damn good.

CHAPTER ELEVEN

The next morning, Lauren came in bright and early. After knocking on the door, she flitted into the room with a tape measure and some material swatches in tow.

"Good morning, dear," she chirped, making Autumn's head hurt. It was way too early to be that happy. But Autumn forced a smile as she dragged herself over to her pile of clothes to snatch up her dress.

"Oh, don't bother," Lauren said as she tried to sneak into the tiny bathroom to change. "I'd just like to get your measurements."

Autumn turned to face the woman, quirking a brow. Measurements?

"Gods know you need a new dress for the festival. That one Kay gave you won't do at all." Lauren beckoned her over. "It'll only take a minute, dear."

Autumn contemplated escape. She really did. What the hell was a festival anyway? And why would she need a new dress for it?

After a moment, she decided she was being silly. Lauren had been a slave like her, and she seemed very empathetic. So, Autumn stepped across the room to stand in front of her.

Lauren smiled and motioned for her to raise her arms, which she obeyed. That was one thing she'd always been good at. Obedience.

"My goodness. You're so tiny, I'll be able to whip up a few dresses in no time," Lauren said as she read the number on the measuring tape wrapped around Autumn's waist. She took a few more measurements as Autumn forced herself to remain still, cringing inside as the tape floated against her skin.

After Lauren set the tape down, she picked up the swatches and beamed at her. "Now, which material do you like best?"

Autumn stared at the woman, gaping. *I... I can choose?* Other than her paintings, she'd never been able to make her own choices in her life. Her clothes had been thrown at her as a guard or someone worse demanded she get dressed...or undressed. Her skin crawled. Thank goodness the measuring part was over.

Autumn shook the dark memories away and concentrated on the swatches. She quickly pointed one out and Lauren smiled brighter. "I was thinking the same thing," she chirped and winked. "Could I call on you later to try it on once I'm finished?"

After Autumn nodded, Lauren collected her things and skipped out the door, leaving her to wonder what kind of dress could possibly make someone that happy?

Today was the day. The Winter Solstice. The festival would start at sundown, and he planned to show Autumn everything she'd been missing. The Winter Solstice festival was his favorite day of the year. The food, the music, the decorations...not to the mention the presents. It was an entire evening of nothing but fun, fun, and more fun. Who wouldn't love it?

He glanced at himself in the mirror that hung behind their large dining table. Not bad for someone that rarely wore clothes with buttons. Or cared much about their appearance in general. His palms were already sweaty. Tonight had to go perfect. No pressure.

Someone cleared their throat, very loudly and obviously, behind him. He knew before he turned around that it had been Kay. His sister beamed at him. "She's ready," she squealed.

Kay and his mum had spent half the day in his room with Autumn. He had no doubt they had made up for all the pampering girly stuff she'd missed in her life. Make that two lifetimes.

"Took you guys long enough," he teased because he couldn't help himself. In truth, he hadn't minded waiting one bit. Autumn deserved every second of pampering and then some.

Kay narrowed her eyes at him, sticking out her tongue as she waltzed down the stairs, her pale blue gown swaying behind her.

And then the world stopped. Autumn had appeared at the top of the stairs, clad in emerald green lace that hugged every curve she possessed. Her bright red hair was pulled back from her face, making her eyes catch each beam of candlelight as she tiptoed down the stairs, clutching the rail.

"Wh... whoa. You look...um...wow."

Kay giggled next to him, amused by his sudden case of the stutters.

But he didn't care because at that moment, Autumn's piercing gaze found his. Before her gaze roamed down his body, heat rising from the dazzling depths. That one tiny hint of approval sent his body into a spiral of desire. Because now he wanted to see her look at him like that all the time. Greedy bastard that he was.

"Gosh, you two. Get a room," Kayline chimed in, pulling Autumn's gaze to the floor as her beautiful freckled cheeks flushed.

He threw his sister a nasty look for ruining such a perfect moment, but she only shrugged at him, trying to hide a smirk and failing epically.

"Where's Pop, anyway?" she asked, glancing around the entryway.

Torin clenched his jaw shut, still harboring ill will towards his old man. He lifted a shoulder but didn't respond.

His mum floated down the stairs a few minutes later, festive as ever in her favorite red satin gown and smiling at the three of them. Then, her gaze flickered behind them. "Well, don't you two look wonderful. I'm glad you decided to join us as well, Nessie, Charlie."

A pit dropped into his stomach at the mention of his other sister's name. And her boyfriend. He turned on his heel, placing his body in front of Autumn's. The couple stood just in front of the basement door where they'd skulked out of. Apparently, his mother had made Nessie a dress as well. A simple gold gown that hugged her hips. Sleeveless. Surprise, surprise. Because her being half-vampire, half-lycana meant she didn't even feel the cold.

He opened his mouth to tell them to beat it.

"Torin," his mother warned.

Snarling under his breath, he took a breath. "Yes, very nice of you to join us."

Nessie raised a brow at him. "Thanks. You couldn't look more thrilled to see us, really."

He gave her a droll look, which she returned.

"Well, we best be going. Don't want to miss the tree lighting," Charlie interjected, holding an elbow out for Nessie. "Shall we?"

Nessie took one look at the formal gesture and rolled her eyes at him. "Oh, yes. Wouldn't want to miss that excitement." And she took off out the door, leaving Charlie to chase after her.

"Well, I like her," Kayline chirped. "It's quite funny seeing someone else get under Torin's skin." She gave him a wide smile and skipped out the door after them.

Torin rolled his eyes before turning on his mother. "Why did you invite the bloodsuckers? And why in the gods' names did you make her a dress? She is your husband's child from another woman!"

His mother bristled, anger flaring in her brown eyes. Her gaze flickered to Autumn, softening before she looked back at him. "Out of respect for Autumn, I will not dignify those ridiculous questions with an answer. I will simply tell you, my dear son, that your new sister has been through every bit as much as that woman you're so protectively guarding." She walked past him, lifting the billowing skirts of her dress in her rush to get away from him. "Nessie deserves a break in her life, too."

It was his turn to blush in embarrassment...and shame. Had he really been that shitty to her? He glanced over at Autumn, who stood wide-eyed and confused. Would she think he was as shitty as he felt right now?

Seeing the questions in her eyes, he said, "Nessie is the bloo...I mean, woman...you met back at Blackmoon."

Autumn swallowed and nodded, so he continued. "She also happens to be my half-sister."

She raised her brows, puckering her lips at him.

"Yeah, I haven't been too thrilled about it."

Her lips curved in a small smirk.

"Anyway, enough about my family tree growing. Let's get to the fun stuff, shall we?" He held his arm out *(just like Charlie, ugh. Hate myself right now)*, but, unlike his prissy sister, Autumn smiled widely and slipped her arm over his.

Autumn couldn't believe her eyes. She had never seen a more beautiful scene in her whole life and her fingers were itching for a paintbrush. Hanging lanterns were scattered throughout the village, a fire crackling in the huge firepit that marked the center. Potted pine saplings formed a wide circle around the pit with shiny colored ornaments of all shapes and sizes. She ran to get closer, yanking Torin's arm.

Miniature sleighs and snowmen hung from the branches along with snowflakes made from yarn. And atop each little tree was a shining white moon, the silhouette of a howling wolf lit from the inside.

Torin finally pulled her away from her admiration of every little decoration by insisting she try some food. She begrudgingly allowed him to lead her towards a long, long table of food. She'd never had much of an appetite. Being in a case of constant fear and disgust usually did that to a person. Besides, she was only ever permitted to eat when someone told her to or brought food to her little room in Blackmoon.

Torin's face, on the other hand, lit up as the feast came into view. Probably much the way her face had just lit up moments ago. He snatched up a large hunk of meat and glanced over at her.

"Take what you want," he said through a mouthful of meat.

She quirked a brow at him. Whatever she wanted?

He waved a hand at the food. "Don't be shy. Here, you gotta try this." He shoved the hunk of meat in her face, making her back away. The smell of it turned her stomach and brought the past screaming to the surface of her mind.

"Autumn," a booming voice called in the darkness as the door of her tiny room creaked open, bringing the stench of blood and sweat into the air. "Where's my pretty girl?"

She tried to hold her breath as she rocked in the corner, hugging her knees to her chest. I'm not here. I'm not here.

"There you are." He chuckled as his dark eyes landed on her. "Trying to hide again, are you?"

He squatted down in front of her, a beefy hand fisting in her hair and yanking her head up. "Silly girl. You can't hide from me." He pulled her head forward making her wince as a chunk of hair tore from her scalp. He closed his eyes, taking a long whiff of her hair. "I could smell you from miles away, my pretty girl."

Autumn kept her eyes on him as he threw her to the floor and climbed on top of her, shoving her filthy dress out of the way. Even as he pushed inside her, she watched on. Because the monster didn't like it when she closed her eyes. If she did, she'd wake up with more than just the junction between her legs screaming in agony. But she couldn't stop the tears as she waited in the wreaking darkness for the monster to be done with her.

Turning away, she ran. And vomited behind the closest building she could find.

Torin followed her, ditching the hunk of meat. But she vomited again, waving him off. "I'm just trying to help," he said, reaching for her.

She flailed her arms harder. *Well, you're not! You're disgusting!*

He threw his arms in the air. "Alright, fine, I'm going!" He spun on his heel and marched away, muttering about confusing women.

When she'd rid herself of the little bit of breakfast she had eaten that morning, she leaned against the side of the building to catch her breath. And trying to remind herself that this wasn't Blackmoon. After finally composing herself, she straightened and inspected the dress that Lauren had made her, praying it wasn't ruined. She'd never owned anything so beautiful in her life. She sighed in relief when she found no damage had been done.

She eyed the food table, but Torin had disappeared. And her appetite was G.O.N.E. But she tiptoed out from behind the building, determined not to cower in the corner. She'd spent her whole goddamn life cowering in a corner!

"I see my son got his way and brought you to the celebration," a curt, male voice came from behind her. Her body ceased immediately, her breath coming in short bursts as fear froze her lungs.

Torin's father came around her and she stared up at him, swallowing down more fear.

"I told him there was no point, but he won't listen to me," he continued. "Not since he brought you here."

Gulp. The contempt on his face made any determination she'd previously had to enjoy herself shrivel up and run back to the corner screaming.

"The world we live in isn't always fair. Your presence here is threatening my pack. My family." His eyes, so like his son's but lacking any kind of warmth when he looked at her, drilled into hers. "That's why you have to go back. I'm sorry. There's no other way."

His words cut through her, taking her breath and making her tremble. He was taking her back. Back to that cell. Back to the monster.

Torin slammed the door shut as he exited the bathroom. He'd washed his hands clean of any food residue. Even though he was still starving. Damn women. There went his perfect first date.

What did you expect? She didn't even know it was a date.

He cursed himself to the moon and back. Until he spotted his father...talking to Autumn. And she looked petrified, her hands pressed over her mouth as she held back tears.

"There's no other way," he heard his father say as he raced over to them, pulling her behind him. She squealed, reminding him that she'd been yanked around enough. He released her arm, mouthing a quick "sorry" at her. But she was shaking her head, her eyes locked onto his as tears finally broke free.

"What did you say to her?" he yelled, turning on his father. Not giving a fuck that his father looked pissed at his tone.

His father composed himself, looking serious, as always. "I told her what you refuse to acknowledge," he stated and walked away.

No, he thought, praying his father wasn't really that cruel. Torin looked back at Autumn. "Don't worry," he began, but she took one look at him and fled towards the house.

Autumn stood staring into the fire once again locked inside Torin's room. Only this time, she'd locked herself in. After a while, she went into the adjoining bathroom to grab a tissue, gasping as she caught sight of her reflection.

There in the mirror was the woman who had haunted her dreams. Long, flowing locks of red. Eyes of jade. And ugly streaks of tears blotching her face.

Before she could contemplate the meaning of that realization, a knock came at the door.

"Can I come in?"

It was Torin.

She couldn't tell him to go away, so all she could do was remain silent. Pretend she wasn't here, or something lame like that.

"Autumn, please."

She bit her lip. Why did he have to go and use her name? It sounded so...wonderful. He made her actually like hearing it. Damn him.

She unlocked the door.

He didn't smile at her this time. Instead, he looked...sad. Like he was the one hurting. And then he looked angry. "My father's an asshole."

He was angry at his father. Not her. Why? Because he'd told her she'd have to return to Blackmoon.

"And he can go fuck himself because I won't let him take you. Over my dead body."

Autumn heard herself gasp just before she launched herself into his arms and sobbed all over again.

Torin clutched her against his body, absorbing her tears like he wished he could absorb her pain.

He put a gentle hand on the back of her head, cooing at her until her body finally stopped shaking with sobs.

When she lifted her head to look at him, he raised his palms to swipe the tears from her face. "Let's try to salvage this night. I promise I won't let the asshole known as my father near you again."

She half-cried, half-laughed as she circled her face with her hands.

He smiled at her. "You still took beautiful to me," he said, winking.

Her cheeks flushed instantly, but she rolled her eyes and disappeared into the bathroom. After some short nose-blows, she came out with a smudge-free face, eyes still a little red and puffy, but that would fade soon enough.

"Perfect," he chimed, holding out his arm for round two.

Once back outside, he found himself eyeing the food table. His stomach must have noticed because it growled in unison.

Autumn glanced over at him, her gaze dropping to his noisy stomach before raising an eyebrow at him. Her plump lips curved into a tiny smile.

He gave her a wide grin. "So, what do you like to eat?"

She thought about it for a minute before shrugging.

"Well, I'll bring you a few things. You try whatever you want, okay?"

She looked surprised, but nodded a moment later, waiting at a distance as he piled food onto a plate. Her eyes watched his every move. He made a point to avoid all meat. Maybe she was a vegetarian or something.

After cautiously inspecting the plate, she peeked up at him through her eyelashes with the slightest hint of a smile. His gut clenched at the haughty, flirtatious look. She picked off a few grapes, popping them inside that pretty mouth one at a time, gauging his reaction.

Good gods, she had no idea how sexy that was. How sexy she was. His face must have given his thoughts away, but instead of looking terrified again, her eyes heated, her mouth parting.

He was almost ready to lean into her when she shoved a huge chunk of buttered bread into her mouth. She grinned at him, cheeks puffed full of food. And he couldn't help but laugh.

But his laughter died as he spotted "the asshole" through the billowing smoke rising over the bonfire. His father stood on the other side of the village center, talking with Nessie's mother, Eva, his palm pressed against the building as he gazed down at her. There was too much noise for Torin to pick up a word they were saying. Then, his father grinned, teeth showing, eyes crinkling. A real smile. One that he had not seen on his father's face in years. The sight of it made Torin seethe, searching the village for the woman his father *should* be laughing with.

Instead, his mother – her mating marks peeking out from beneath her fur shawl - and sister, Kay, were talking and laughing over some steaming cups of cocoa. They hadn't seemed to take notice of his father. Or his company.

Eva laid a hand on his father's arm, gazing up at him with such longing on her face it made Torin want to gag on his festive pudding pie.

And then a hand rested on his own arm, pulling his attention away from his two-timing father. Autumn looked up at him with concern, her own eyes darting over to his father and Eva.

"Yeah," he muttered. "The asshole's batting a thousand today."

Concern turned to confusion as she tilted her head and quirked a brow.

He shook his head. "Nevermind, I don't want to talk about it."

She patted his arm and motioned for him to continue.

He pulled his arm away. "I said I don't want to talk about it, okay."

Snatching her hand back against her chest, she pressed her lips together as she stared up at him with wide eyes filled with apprehension.

Luckily, the tree lighting ceremony began a moment later, overshadowing his quick snap at her and saving the moment in a flash of bright colors that had her eyes lighting up every bit as beautifully as the tree.

CHAPTER TWELVE

It had been over a week since Torin had brought her to his home. Rescued her from hell and introduced her to what she could only assume was actual happiness. It was a foreign feeling, but one she could get used to in a hurry. Each morning she seemed to wake up earlier, anxious to start the day and see everyone's smiling faces. Well, except Talon's. Because his was never smiling. Ever. At least not when she was around.

But even as she flitted about the house like a happy little harpy, deep in the pit of her stomach she knew it couldn't last. Talon had been very blunt with her at the festival. Her time here was limited, and her days numbered. Still, she was determined to enjoy it while it lasted. She'd need these happy memories to keep her sanity back in Blackmoon.

Her heart ached every time she thought about returning to that personal corner of hell. But that was a worry for another day. Today, she was taking her painting supplies into the village, finally putting the vision that was the Winter Solstice festival onto a canvas.

She spent ten minutes picking the perfect spot to set up. Because lighting was crucial, of course. Then, she settled in for a few hours of her favorite past time. Torin probably wouldn't be back from his hunting trip until dusk anyway. In no time, her mind was completely immersed in the task of getting every detail right. Torin who?

"Oh, my stars," someone gasped behind her, startling her. Not that it took much. "That is spectacular!"

Autumn turned to smile at Lauren's kind words.

"I had no idea you were so talented, dear." Lauren gazed at her artwork for several more seconds, shaking her head in amazement.

Then, the woman jerked, her eyes lighting up as she looked at Autumn. "That would be perfect for you. An art teacher! Oh, sometimes I think I'm a genius. Wait until I tell the children!"

Autumn gaped after her as she skipped through the village and out of sight. Art teacher? Her? She must be joking, right? what did she know about children? Let alone teaching them.

She pushed the notion from her mind as she returned to her work. No matter. As intriguing as the idea sounded, she probably wouldn't be here long enough to actually participate in this teaching thing anyway. Or so she thought...

It only took a few minutes before children from all over the village came bustling through the previously quiet street. Lauren trailed behind them, huffing and puffing to keep up.

"Children, children, settle down," she demanded coming to stand beside Autumn. And the children listened. This woman had some magic up her sleeves or something. No woman she'd ever encountered had wielded such unquestionable power before. "Everyone, this is Miss Autumn."

"Good morning, Miss Autumn," the children sang in unison as they all smiled up at her.

"Now, Autumn doesn't say much, but I'd like you to watch her for a few minutes while she paints. Watch carefully, though. Because one day very soon, I'll be having all of you try to paint something as pretty as Autumn's picture." She held up a finger, her face turning serious. "But only if you behave yourselves, am I understood?"

"Yes, Mrs. Delaney."

Autumn stared at the children as they stared up at her with curious faces. Lauren laid a hand on her arm. "It's okay, dear. They're going to love watching you paint, I'm sure of it."

Gazing up at Lauren's hopeful face had Autumn pressing her lips together and nodding. She didn't want to disappoint the woman who apparently had so much faith in her ability to keep the attention of a dozen small children.

A few miles outside the village, Torin crouched in the thick bushes, his fingers grasping the handle of his bow a little too tight. His father knelt next to him in an identical position. Alaric and Jarden, another Whitemoon Warrior, hid in the bushes across the path. They'd been out hunting since this morning and their wagon was only half full. Where the hell was everything? The forest was eerily quiet. As if the animals sensed the uneasiness in the area.

"Something's not right," he muttered. "We should have had twice as many catches two hours ago. It's past sundown. We've been at this all fucking day."

Nodding, his father whispered back, "I know. Must be all the tension spreading."

He glared over at his father, hearing the accusation in his tone. Tension was certainly spreading. Even now, he could feel it in the air between the two of them. He had crouched next to his father during hunting trips countless times in his life. Hell, the man had taught him almost everything he knew.

.

Twelve years earlier...

.

"Torin, pay attention!"

He snapped his head up, straightening his spine as he met his father's gaze.

His father paced in front of him, along with a dozen other boys. "Since you don't feel the need to listen, I assume you're ready for battle, eh son?"

Torin gulped down a lump in his throat before nodding.

Talon looked down at him with the tiniest hint of a smile. "You think you can take down the enemy, then?"

He nodded again, looking straight ahead. "Yes, sir."

Crouching in front of him, his father quirked a brow and smiled at him. "I like your confidence. But, the real question is...can you take me down?"

Torin's gaze flickered to his father's face, and he let out a sigh of relief at the twinkle of amusement in his father's eye. He drew his wooden sword, waggling his eyebrows. "Bring it on, old man."

His father grabbed a wooden sword of his own and the two began to circle one another. After several swings and misses, his father chuckled, swatting the flat side of his sword across Torin's backside. "Is this old man too quick for you, boy?"

Just behind his father, he caught sight of Alaric snatching a wooden sword from the pile and winking at him.

"Not really," he said to his father, twirling out of reach. "Just wanted to give your old bones a chance to catch up."

His father gave a hearty laugh as he parried Torin's thrust. "Just remember, your enemies won't hesitate to gut you while you're cracking jokes."

Torin gave his father a wide smile. "I know."

Alaric jabbed the sword into his father's back, making his father spin on his heel. Torin took his chance, jumping onto his father's back and slicing the dull sword across his father's throat.

"You lose, old man."

His father feigned a groan and fell to his knees.

"That wasn't fair," one of the other boys shouted. "You and Alaric cheated. It was supposed to be one-on-one."

Torin and Alaric crossed their arms over their chests. "There is no fair play in battle. Only life and death," they spoke together, quoting the words of his father.

His father laid a hand on his shoulder, beaming down at him. "Well played, son."

.

A twig cracked up the path and they both pulled their bowstrings taught in preparation for the coming kill.

Instead of a deer or boar, a group of another kind of wild pigs came down the path. Blackmoon Warriors. Six of them. Fan-fucking-tastic.

He and his father glanced at each other, communicating with a single look. *Well, they are in our territory.* And Torin didn't need much of an excuse to wipe these fuckers off the face of the Earth.

Jarden and Alaric peeked through the bushes at them, and his father gave them a stiff nod, counting down on his fingers. Three. Two. One.

They leapt from the bushes, each targeting a different enemy. But they were expecting it, swords clashing in a scream of metal-on-metal. Torin smiled to himself, already soaking in the adrenaline. Time to find out if these bastards could fight like men instead of the dogs they were.

Turns out. They could. Dammit.

Though Torin could tell his own men clearly out skilled Blackmoon, the enemy outnumbered them. When Jarden stumbled, and almost got gutted, Torin decided it was time to go. Better to go back and get reinforcements.

Before he could signal the others, two more bodies fell from the trees.

"What the fuck!" Alaric yelled as two of the Blackmoon Warriors roared. Each of them now sporting a leech on their back and the bitemarks to match.

"Bloodsuckers!" one of the Blackmoon Warriors screamed as he watched his brother-in-arms flail at the intrusion.

"Fuck this," another one of them snapped, taking off in the direction they came. The other leechless cowards followed suit.

The bloodsuckers released their victims as soon as the others were well out of sight. The female one smirked up at him, blood still dripping from the side of her mouth. "You're welcome."

Torin rolled his eyes, sighing.

Alaric chuckled beside him. "Your sister certainly knows how to make an entrance."

Jarden wasn't as amused, cursing at the two of them. "Filthy bloodsuckers. We didn't need your help."

Charlie stood there looking bored with the whole thing, but not Nessie. Oh, no. Of course not.

She tilted her head at the two others, raising her eyebrows. "From where I was standing, you were about to get gutted." She snapped her fangs at Jarden. "And if anyone calls me a fucking bloodsucker one more time, I'll give you a mark to match those Blackmoon cowards."

Torin caught a smirk flicker across his father's face.

Jarden snarled at her, pulling Charlie's attention. He bared his fangs at the other male in a clear warning. Don't threaten his girl. Period.

"Fuck you, she started it," he snapped.

Alaric laughed. "Really, Jar? How old are you? Twelve?"

"That's enough," his father snapped.

Jarden clamped his mouth shut, then flipped Alaric the finger.

Alaric blew him a kiss.

"You should try to get along with the pack members better, Nessie," his father said, sliding his sword back into the sheath at his hips.

Nessie snorted at him. "Who'd want to be friends with that asshole?"

"Who'd want to be friends with a bloodsucking bitch like you?" Jarden growled.

Nessie leaped for him, fangs bared. Fortunately, Charlie knew her well and anticipated it, wrapping his arms around her waist and holding her back. It was obviously a struggle because he was losing ground.

"I told him not to call me a fucking bloodsucker!"

His father stepped in front of Nessie. "Save it for Blackmoon. He's on our side whether you like it or not."

"And he didn't call her a bloodsucker, technically," Torin said, turning to Nessie. "He called you a bloodsucking bitch. Gotta admit, he has a point. You do suck blood, and you can be kind of a bitch."

Nessie stopped struggling as she glared over at him. "You're an asshole."

Torin shrugged. "Well, you're a bitch. So, we're even."

"Torin," his father growled in warning.

Nessie shoved Charlie's hands away, coming up to his face. "Guess it runs in the family then."

Torin narrowed his gaze on her. The stark reminder that she was, in fact, related to him made him clench his fists as he glanced at his father. Nessie had been here less than a month, but his father had welcomed all of them without hesitation. Without even thinking about how it affected his family. The one he had before they showed up.

He sneered at her. "You're *not* my family. You're just the bastard daughter of my father."

He turned to head back to the village, hearing Nessie start to struggle against Charlie again. A heavy hand fell on his shoulder. He glanced back, the disappointment in his father's eyes burning a hole through his heart. He shrugged his father's hand away and headed off into the woods alone. Alaric fell into step beside him a few moments later.

"You wanna..."

"Nope."

When Torin finally pulled the wagon alongside the butcher's shack hours later, the moon had finally crested over the treetops, illuminating the village in its eerie glow. Torin stretched his arms over his head as he walked back towards his house. His skin was starting to feel too tight. It always did when the full moon was close.

And with all the bad blood boiling between the packs lately, not to mention within the village - hell his own house - this full moon was gonna be a doozy.

He contemplated going for an evening run to stretch his legs in preparation for the full moon shift but decided against it. He'd spent all day in those damn woods today. And if he was being honest with himself, he was dying to see Autumn. It felt like he hadn't laid eyes on her for ages. *Gods, I'm becoming pathetic.*

He opened the front door, heading into the kitchen instead of heading straight upstairs. Might as well grab some grub on the way.

He passed his mother as she stood stirring a pot on the stove. Opening the cupboard, he snatched a pack of jerky off the shelf. "What's for dinn---Mum?"

His mother stood in a daze, stirring the pot as if on autopilot.

"Mum?" Stepping towards her, he placed his hand on the one she rested on the counter.

She jumped, gasping and almost knocking the pot off the stove. He caught it, hissing as the heat blistered his skin. Ignoring it, he set the pot right again. "Mum, what's wrong?"

She shook her head, fluttering her hand over her chest. "Nothing. Nothing. I guess I'm just a little jumpy right now with ---ummm---nevermind."

"With what? What is it?"

Kayline came swooping into the room, carrying a basket of berries. "Holy shit," she whispered. "That guy really is fucking scary-looking."

Torin gave her a wary look. "What guy?"

His sister's icy-blue eyes met his. "Blackmoon's Alpha."

"What the fuck were you doing near Blackmooon?"

She furrowed her brows, her hand slamming onto her hip. "I wasn't, asshole. He's here. In Pop's office."

"What?!"

Torin flew through the house, slamming the door to his father's office open.

His father sat in his usual chair in front of his large desk. And lounging in the chair across from him was Jaxon Bearpaw.

"What the fuck is he doing here?"

"Torin," his father growled.

Jaxon, the giant beast of a man, chuckled at him. "I admire your son's...bluntness, Talon."

He doubted that highly. This sick puppy didn't admire anything but his own twisted self. He could see it in the way he carried himself. Straight, chest out. Using every bit of his seven-foot-plus height to his advantage. Torin dwarfed next to him, not even six-foot himself.

"Torin, this is..." his father began.

"I fucking know who he is," Torin snapped. "What is he doing here?"

Jaxon's wide mouth expanded, teeth shining at him in an evil grin. "I've come to negotiate the return of the slave girl you stole from me."

Torin clenched his jaw at the mention of Autumn. Especially being called "slave girl." She'd never be that again if he had anything to do with it.

"I don't know what you're talking about," he muttered, looking at the door for his escape.

"Oh, I know it was you," Jaxon sneered, standing from the chair. "I could smell her all over you the moment you walked in here." His sneer flipped into an evil grin. "And, trust me, I know what she smells like."

Motherfucker. "You'll never get your meaty paws on her again," Torin snarled.

He snickered. "Unfortunately for you, she's mine."

Torin took those last steps toward the giant. "Not anymore."

Jaxon raised a brow as he snickered again. "Either return what's mine or deliver to me another female in exchange. I will accept no one older than her current age. And I reserve the right to deny any substitution upon closer inspection."

"We don't have slaves," Torin said, narrowing his eyes.

Jaxon smiled. "I'll give you one week to decide. Consider it a kindness after your unwarranted attack last week."

"You kidnapped one of our member's mate. We were completely within our right to retrieve him. Under any circumstances," Talon stated, stepping around his desk.

Jaxon shook his head, sneering. "Mating with bloodsuckers now. That's low even for your pack, Talon."

Despite his feelings towards his father at the moment, he wasn't about to let this dickhead insult him. He tilted his head towards Jaxon, getting the dickhead's attention. "I heard the female one did quite a number on you. How's the ribs feeling today, asshole?" Because he'd heard talk that Nessie had kicked the shit out of them during their attack, knocking the cocky son of a bitch out cold.

Jaxon growled at him, taking a long stride towards him as his father came between them.

"That's enough," his father shouted, throwing his arms out.

"Save it, Pop. I was on my way out anyway."

He left the den with a hard pit of determination in his stomach. He headed straight for the shower before he went to reassure himself that Autumn was still in his room. He wanted to wash the stench of animal carcasses off him. She probably wouldn't appreciate that particular aroma. And he needed to at least smell inviting. Because, tonight, he wasn't leaving her side. Not with that beast in the same house. What the fuck was his father thinking?!

CHAPTER
THIRTEEN

Something was off. Autumn could tell as soon as she opened the door to find Torin staring at her with a mixture of worry and anger. Which confused the shit out of her, but she said nothing. Because that's what she always did. And it was beginning to get a little annoying. Her questions always went unanswered because she didn't actually ask them. Stupid vow of silence.

"Mind if I come in?" he asked, even though he was already stepping through the door.

Rolling her eyes, she nodded, but he wasn't paying attention. Yeah, something felt very off. Most of the time his eyes were glued to her whenever he was around her. Which should have creeped her out, but she found it oddly comforting.

His head was shaking as he sighed to himself over and over. Clearly agitated about something. She put her hand on his arm, drawing his attention. Finally. Good gods, was she really that desperate for his attention? She gave him a concerned look.

Shaking his head, he muttered. "It's nothing. I'm fine." He pulled his face together, planting a smile on it. The fakest smile she'd ever seen on his face. "So, what are you painting tonight?"

She smiled at him, hoping it might bring him out of whatever funk he was in. Walking over to another canvas set up in front of the fireplace, she showed him her latest project. It was the Winter Solstice piece she'd started that morning. The children had been a slight distraction, so she hadn't finished it as early as she'd planned. She'd wanted to give it to him as a gift, but she hadn't finished it in time.

His face brightened, his phony smile replaced with a real one. "Your talent still amazes me every time I see it."

Blushing, she nodded in thanks.

As he'd done for the past few nights, he sat with her as she painted, chatting about his day. Only tonight, he kept pausing, stopping himself from finishing a sentence, and then quickly changing the subject. Eventually, she got up from her chair to stretch and headed for the door.

He planted himself in the doorway. "Where are you going? Do you need something?"

She furrowed her brows. What was his problem tonight? She mimed drinking, and he nodded, holding his palms up.

"Let me get it for you. I'll bring us some hot tea. Just stay here and relax," he threw her a hurried grin as he shut the door and she heard him scurry down the hallway. She blinked at the door, wondering what could have gotten him so worked up. She grabbed the doorknob, checking to see it if had been locked. It hadn't. Of course. She had to stop being so paranoid.

Not really wanting to stay in the room by herself pacing, she moseyed down the hallway, intending to help Torin with the tea. Instead, she heard shouting from the bedroom at the other end of the hall. And she just couldn't stop herself from being nosy.

"How dare you, Talon Delaney! How dare you make our son take that poor girl back there!"

"Now, Lauren. I cannot have us going to war over one slave girl," Talon said calmly.

Lauren bristled. "She is a person, you...you jackwagon! I thought you understood that, or are you just like all those other Alphas? Who see us humans as things instead of people? To be traded and thrown around at your whim."

"You don't understand, woman! Blackmoon will overrun us if they gain support from the other packs."

"That is not the point, and you know it!"

"Then what is the point?" he yelled back.

"You banned slavery for a reason, Talon. Or don't you remember why?"

He huffed. "Of course, I remember. But she is not my wife, and she isn't part of my pack."

"Neither was I once upon a time. I was a slave. In Blackmoon, you pompous jerk!" She jabbed at his chest, raising on her tiptoes as she shoved her face as close to his as she could get it. "That girl is absolutely no different than I am. And I swear to the gods, Talon. If you send her back there, I will go to Blackmoon myself. And if I make it back alive, trust me, you will have a war on your hands."

"You would risk your life for that girl?" he asked, his eyes wide with disbelief.

"Thank the gods your son has more compassion than you do, Talon Delaney. I won't let him lose her because of your cowardice."

His gaze narrowed, his nose scrunching in anger. Autumn clamped her hands over her mouth to stifle the gasp. She'd just called him a coward...to his face?! No fear. Just brutal honesty. That woman was her hero.

Lauren stepped through the door, jumping as she turned toward her. "Oh! My dear, you have become quite the eavesdropper, haven't you? No doubt I can blame those children of mine for teaching you their bad habits."

Tears stung her eyes as her throat clenched. The kindest woman she'd ever met had just took on her own husband. A man twice her size. All for Autumn. She'd never felt anything like it before. This sense of safety. The reality of having others care for her well-being was completely foreign to her. Not since her own mother had something bothered to protect her. And, from what she could recall, her own mother had been too sick and frail to do much protecting. If anything, Autumn had protected her more than the other way around.

She threw her arms around Lauren's neck, weeping into her shoulders.

"Oh, dear. I'm so sorry you had to hear my husband say those things." Lauren stroked her hair. "You aren't going anywhere. Not if I have any say in it."

Autumn shook her head, sniffling as she lifted her head and gazed into Lauren's kind eyes. "Thank you," she whispered, her voice cracking.

Lauren smiled at her with tears forming in her own eyes as well. "Oh. My dear girl," she said, pulling Autumn back into an embrace. "You are most welcome."

"What's going on?" Torin's voice pulled Autumn from Lauren's arms. She wiped her tears away hastily. Why, she had no idea. Not like the man hadn't seen her cry before.

Lauren cleared her throat. "Poor Autumn just overheard me and your father arguing. That's all."

Torin narrowed his gaze on his mother. "What were you arguing about?"

"Never you mind. That's none of your business."

"Was it about her? If so, then it is my business."

A hint of a smile broke across Lauren's face, but she quickly composed herself. "Fine. It's probably best you know anyway. Your father plans on giving Autumn back to Blackmoon. I just ran into him and---" She shivered, struggling to continue. "Jaxon discussing the situation."

Autumn gasped, smashing a hand over her mouth as her eyes widened. Jaxon? Was here? IN THIS HOUSE? Shaking her head, she backed away, turning to flee back to Torin's room.

Torin's jaw ticked before he caught sight of her. He placed a gentle hand on her arm, but she flailed at the touch. "It's okay, Autumn. I told you I wouldn't let him take you."

But she was still shaking her head before she turned tail and ran. Luckily, she was headed back to his own room. He breathed a sigh of relief. Well, he was headed there anyway with their tea in tow. He looked back at his mother.

"Pop told me the day I brought her back that she couldn't stay. He's actually given me longer than he originally said. But now Jaxon has put an official deadline on it. We have one week."

His mother shook his head as tears welled in her sad, brown eyes. "We can't let her go back there. We just can't."

He threw an arm around his mother, knowing now how this must bring back painful memories. "I won't let them take her. I can't."

She smiled up at him through her tears. "I know she means a lot to you, dear. I hope she knows that, too." She patted his cheek as she stepped out of his arms. "You go make sure our girl is safe. She deserves to be happy. You both do."

"Thanks, Mum," he said, giving the well-deserving woman a quick hug.

She squeezed him back. "I love you, dear."

"Love you, too," he muttered, pecking her on the cheek and heading back towards his room. Before the tea got as cold as his father's heart was lately. And to think he used to look up to the man.

When he got back to his room, he found Autumn rocking in the corner behind his bed. He frowned as he set the two mugs of tea on the bedside table. Jaxon Bearpaw had done this. Turned her into this frightened woman who couldn't even hear his name without shaking (literally) with fear. Couldn't handle the touch of another man for fear of being hurt. Couldn't speak for fear her voice may cause her pain. He had never laid eyes on a more damaged human being. It made his heart ache and his blood boil. Wanting to cause just as much damage to the man --- NO, the beast--- who did this to her.

"Autumn," he called softly, but she clamped her hands over her ears, rocking harder. Shit, why did he have to sound like a man right now?

"Autumn," he called again, raising his pitch as high as it would go. He sounded ridiculous, but it got her to stop rocking. He called her again in the ridiculous, high-pitched voice.

She lifted her head, looking around with confused eyes. As if searching for another person.

"No, it's me," he said in the funny voice again.

She quirked a brow as she scanned his face.

"Well, if this is the only way you'll talk to me, then I guess I have to sound like a complete clown," he said.

Her mouth fell open as her hands fell away from her ears. She shook her head at him.

"What? You don't like the way I sound? Well, that makes two of us, gorgeous."

She shook her head again slowly, her eyes still glued to his face.

"Can I talk normally now?"

Her throat moved as she swallowed hard. But she nodded a second later.

He sighed, his pitch dropping back to normal. "Oh, thank gods. That was hurting my own ears."

She stared at him a moment longer, shaking her head in amazement, just before she closed her eyes and laughed at him. Music to his ears. And worth every moment of making an ass out of himself.

"Look, I'm not sure how you're going to feel about this. But I need to stay in here with you tonight, okay?"

Her laughter stopped as she pointed at the room and the two of them.

He nodded. "Yes, both of us will be sleeping in here tonight. I understand if that makes you uncomfortable. I'm sorry, but with ---ummm---the Blackmoon Alpha nearby, it's the only way I'll know you're safe."

She studied him for a moment, her eyes roaming over his face. Then, out of nowhere, she put her palm on his cheek, nodding her head.

He put her hand over hers, smiling at her. "I'm glad you agree."

They drank their tea by the fireplace where Torin told her all about the Blackmoon warriors he'd fought earlier that day. He even gave Nessie the credit she deserved for swooping in and *cough* saving them. Not that he'd *ever* tell his half-sister that.

She fell asleep listening to him banter on, her body curled on the rug in front of the fireplace, mug still clutched in her tiny hand. He smiled down at her as he swept the stray piece of hair from her face. After covering her with a blanket, he climbed into his bed. He normally slept naked, but he made sure to keep his t-shirt and boxers in place tonight. Autumn didn't need that nasty shock first thing in the morning.

And thank gods he did. Because the next morning, he woke up to find the woman who'd occupied his dreams that night, sleeping right there next to him. Her wild curls splayed across his pillows as she snored softly into the comforter. His heart skipped a beat to see her laying there. In his bed. With him still in it. Miracles do come true.

When Autumn woke the next morning, she could hear Torin in the shower. She really should try that shower thing out. She hadn't been willing to get naked that long, but maybe today was the day. She probably needed it. Sponge-bathing only got you so clean.

She pushed the comforter off her, stretching in the big bed and sighing at how good that simple pleasure felt. Then, she froze. Wait, why was she in his bed?

She'd fallen asleep on the rug last night. She was sure of it. So, how did she end up in the bed? Did he put her there?

She mentally smacked herself as the hazy memory came back to her. No, he hadn't put her there. She'd put herself there. After waking up from one of her signature nightmares, for some reason, she'd wanted to be close to him. But why?

Well, he did say he wanted to make sure you're safe.

Autumn nodded, agreeing with herself. That was true. Torin had only intruded on her privacy for her safety. That must be it then. Safety. *I mean, what else could it be?*

Then, she caught a glimpse of Torin in the bathroom mirror. Because he'd left the door wide open. And her breath hitched. Scratch that, she'd forgotten how to breathe, period.

A towel hung low on his hips, the hard ridges of his abs accentuated by the sharp v-curve of his hipbones. A little trail of dusky-colored hair dipped into the towel and out of sight. And Autumn found herself wanting to know where that little trail led.

The little voice in her head snickered. *What else could it be, indeed.*

Somehow, she found herself leaning against the doorframe of the bathroom, staring at the mirror with wide, hungry eyes. She needed to douse the flames in the hearth because it was getting way too hot in here. And yet, despite the heat, her body shivered. What was going on with her?

Torin's hazel eyes found hers in the reflection of the mirror, locking together in the steamy room. For long moments, they just stared at each other. Unmoving. Eyes darkening with every second.

"You are even more gorgeous in the morning," he murmured in a low, husky voice, breaking the heated silence.

Autumn blinked, trying to get her mind to focus on anything but Torin's half-naked body. And the droplets running down his chest. What she'd give to be one of those droplets.

She shook herself, finally pulling her gaze away. Where did that come from? Torin was a friend. A protector. That was it. Why in the world would she want anything more?

Torin walked over to stand right in front of her. Still clad in his towel...and nothing else. Good gods, she was about to hyperventilate as the smell of him engulfed her in heaven. So fresh. So clean. So delicious. Seriously, *what* was wrong with her?

Torin gazed down at her with those dreamy eyes of every color. A giant smirk planted on his smug face. "Did you need something?"

She cleared her throat. Focus, woman. Focus. She pointed a hand at the toilet behind him. A shaking hand. *Damn it to Hades, pull yourself together!*

Torin nodded. "Ah, of course." He brushed past her, his bare chest rubbing against her arm. The small contact felt like fire licking up her arm, scorching any chance she had of focusing.

She found herself following him as he moved into the bedroom, pulling clothes from his dresser and throwing them onto the bed. He glanced up at her, quirking a brow. His smirk still firmly in place. "The bathroom's open. In case you haven't noticed."

Oh, right. Her bladder needed attention. So did other areas of that body region apparently. Which made no sense. She hated sex. Obviously. It was a smelly, sweaty, painful experience that she had endured because she'd had no choice. There was no way she would choose to do the dirty deed. No way. No. Way.

But as the day wore on, each touch of his hand, each heated look, each husky whisper of his voice sent waves of desire coursing through her. He caught her staring at his scrumptious-looking lips on more than one occasion. It was getting ridiculous really, but she seemed to have no control of her thoughts. No matter what she did, they always circled back to him. And his made-to-kiss mouth. The image of his half-naked body seemed to be permanently seared to her brain.

And Torin was, of course, eating up every second of appreciation. She tried to hide it, but it was useless. She'd never actually appreciated anything about the opposite sex before. So, how was she to know how to hide it?

CHAPTER FOURTEEN

Torin was giddy. Fucking giddy. Until today, he hadn't even been sure Autumn was capable of being attracted to him. Or any man for that matter. But after their little encounter in the bathroom this morning, he had no doubt. She had taken in every inch of his naked torso. And she had liked it. He'd seen her bright eyes darken, following the lines of his body. Hell, she'd licked her lips and probably hadn't even realized it. He was riding on cloud nine as he walked through the village with her.

But as seconds turned to minutes and minutes turned to hours, Torin could feel the dark clouds rolling in to rain all over his good fortune. Because tonight...was the full moon.

The village always got a little crazy this time of the month. Thanks in large part to every lycan beneath its luminous rays shifting with its rise. And unlike other nights, tonight there would be no choice in the matter. And no shifting back until dawn.

He glanced down at Autumn as they walked hand-in-hand through the buzzing village. He'd been sneaking little brushes of contact all day to test her tolerance. No flinching. No quick drawbacks. No jumping ten feet away. If anything, she was beginning to lean into his "accidental" brushes. So, at last, he'd plucked up the courage to take her hand in his own. And she hadn't yanked it back out. Awww, sweet progress.

Kayline stopped to chat with them as she carried a basketful of wild nuts and berries.

"You really shouldn't go out in the woods alone, Kay." Torin knew she'd been out alone by the state of her soiled dress and the fact that Mum wasn't loping along after her with another basket. He hardly ever saw Kayline outside the house without Mum or Pop with her. "They've already snuck into our territory more than once. I wouldn't put it past them to resort to kidnapping women from our village."

Kayline rolled her eyes at him and shooed off his worried with a flick of her wrist. "It's a walk in the woods, not a bush party. Besides, I'm fine, as you can see."

Torin gave her a stern look. "Now, Kay,"

But she shoved a finger in his face. "Don't you 'Now, Kay' me. That's all you and Mum and Pop ever do is boss me around and smother me. I am not a child anymore, for Zeus' sake! I am an adult now whether you all want to accept it or not. And I don't need a goddamn babysitter!" With that, she turned on her heel and stalked toward the house.

He stared after his "little" sister. Unbeknownst to her, she was actually older than he was. Male lycans tended to mature faster than their human counterparts. By ten, he'd been fully matured. And by twelve, he'd been inducted into the Whitemoon Warriors. He'd made his first kill at thirteen. Bed his first woman at fourteen. Broken more than a few hearts by sixteen. At just shy of eighteen, he'd had a lifetime of experiences.

It was probably a good thing Kayline had no clue of their true ages. Otherwise, Mum and Pop would be in for the fight of their lives. In a way, he felt sorry for his "little" sister. Sheltered and protected her whole life, she'd had so few chances to really get out and make friends. Autumn was probably the first friend she'd made around her own age.

He glanced down, seeing Autumn trying to hide a smile. "I take it you agree with her, then?"

Her eyebrows raised as her smile faded. She mulled it over for a few seconds before shrugging her shoulders.

He led her back inside the house as the afternoon sun began to inch closer to the treetops.

"It's best you stay in here tonight."

Autumn didn't argue about it, just nodded at him with wide frightened eyes.

When he turned to leave, she wrapped a hand around his arm, shaking her head. She tried to tug him back away from the door.

Frowning, he stated, "You want me stay with you?"

She didn't hesitate as she nodded, wrapping herself around him in a tight embrace. He closed his eyes as he hugged her back, loving the feel of her body flush against his own. He'd been fighting an erection around her all day. And that was just holding her hand. Now, with her body pressed against him, there was no controlling his own body's response.

Finally, after relishing the blissful moment, he pulled back enough to run his fingers over her cheeks as she stared up at him. He could lose himself forever in those deep pools of jade. "I wish I could," he whispered.

Her fingers clamped down on his arm as he pulled away.

"I...I want to," he continued, forcing himself to peel her off of him. Her need for him was eating through his resistance. An invisible string pulling him back to her. He could see the genuine fear on her face. She knew what the full moon meant. And she wanted him to protect her. Dear gods, he wished he could.

But he didn't trust himself. While his kind didn't lose all sense of self during the shift, their inhibitions were severely compromised. Their basic and primal needs took precedence. And Autumn lit up his libido like a matchstick.

He shook his head as he back away from her, the tears glistening in her frightful eyes like a knife to the heart.

Stay, stay with her. That little voice inside him whispered, tugging that string to bring him back to her.

"No," he murmured. "I... can't."

And despite everything inside him telling him to stay, he fled.

Autumn sat in the corner of the room, rocking as tears slid down her cheeks. He left her. After all this time. All those moments of him wanting to get closer, he chose now, tonight of all nights, to abandon her.

She glanced at the window, seeing the last rays of sun get swallowed up by the impending night. Dusk had fallen. If she recalled from last month, the moon would rise in about an hour. And then the monsters would be out to play.

And she was left to rock in the corner of a room alone. Again. Sniffling, she swiped at her wet face. Screw that. Not this time.

She was tired of being left alone to shake in fear, wondering when the next attack would come. This wasn't Blackmoon. She wasn't a slave here.

Picking her sorry ass up from the floor, she marched out the door. Someone was going to get a piece of her mind. Screw her vow of silence.

Downstairs, she heard voices coming from Talon's den.

"I can't find Kay," Lauren screeched, and Autumn could hear pacing inside the room. "It's nearly moonrise. Where is she?"

Talon growled. "She knows the rules. You both remain inside during the full moon. No exceptions."

Lauren flicked a hand through the air. "Of course she knows that! She's been getting locked in her room every full moon since she was three years old."

"Then, why isn't she here?" Talon snapped.

"Something's going on with her. She's been sneaking off more and more often this past year. And now this."

"Too rebellious. You shouldn't have babied her so much."

"Don't you blame me for this!"

Autumn shook her head as she forced herself to move on. She wasn't down here to eavesdrop. For once. She rounded into the kitchen, halting in her tracks as she spotted who she'd been looking for.

There he stood, clad in only a pair of leather pants as he shoved a half-eaten sandwich into his mouth. He'd abandoned her for a fucking sandwich!

But as he reached to put a loaf of bread back in a high cupboard, her anger dissipated like a wisp. His muscles flexed with each movement as he tidied up the counter, captivating her, flushing her with heat. She never knew that simply watching someone could make her feel like this.

Imagine what doing more than watching could do.

And then he turned, catching her in the act. Again. His eyes hooded, darkening as their gazes locked.

"You shouldn't be down here," he whispered, his voice sending shivers through her. Another wave of heat swept over her in response.

He took a step toward her. But it looked to be a struggle to stop himself. "You need to get back upstairs."

Her name on his lips did strange things to her. There was no way she was going back upstairs. Not without him.

He took another step, clenching his fists at his sides. "I'm not kidding. Get upstairs."

She shook her head at him but never took her greedy eyes from his.

Another step. "Autumn," he growled.

He was struggling not to get too close. Which meant he wanted to get close. He'd been wanting to get close to her for days. Holding her hand. Touching her cheek.

And she wanted his protection. Especially tonight. With monsters roaming right outside the door. And if getting close was what it took to keep him with her through this night, then so be it. She knew what she needed to do.

What you want to do, you mean.

Autumn took those last few steps, closing the distance between them with lightning speed. Confusion flitted across his face, his mouth parting ever-so-slightly as he gaped at her purposeful steps.

Perfect invitation.

She grasped the back of his head with one hand, raising on her toes as she pulled his open mouth down on hers.

A million times she'd been kissed in her lifetime. But none of them had prepared her for the perfection that was Torin's lips. Soft and firm at the same time, his breath catching as her lips latched onto his. He smelled amazing. He felt even better.

And then the flood gates opened.

She may have started the kiss, but he swiftly took over. Pressing his mouth more firmly against hers, he wrapped her up in his arms. Her free hand splayed across his bare chest, the feel of his fevered skin like a beacon to her starving senses.

He groaned as he slid his tongue across her lip, sending a shockwave of lust straight to her core. His mastered mouth tried to coax her lips open, and gods help her, she complied. She found her fingers clenching in his hair of their own accord and he growled inside her mouth. Liquid heat pooled and she had the urge to rub herself against his leathered thigh. This nagging need was foreign to her. She never wanted to be touched. Never.

But now, with a single kiss, she wanted his hands all over her. In every secret place.

In a flash of movement, his hands slid down her back, clenching her bottom as he swept her over to the counter and set her on it.

Her body seemed to have its own agenda, but she didn't mind right now. Her legs wrapped around his hips. His chiseled abs pressed against her, ringing a soft moan from her as it appeased her. Oh, but it sparked a whole new whirlwind of need inside her. More. She needed more of whatever this was.

CHAPTER FIFTEEN

Unbelievable. There were no other words to describe the all-consuming nature of this moment. He wouldn't have believed it if it hadn't just happened in front of his own eyes. And mouth. And everything. Autumn was the world's most unexpected seductress. Her lips had taken his with a force he wouldn't have expected from her.

And it was only getting better. He'd wanted to be gentle, slow and steady wins the race. But his body was having none of that. And, by some miracle, she was giving every bit of it back to him. Her nails clawed down his chest as he pulled her hips towards him, his erection was pressing painfully against the counter's edge, but he didn't care right now.

When she moaned into his mouth, a tidal wave of undiluted lust slaked through him. He opened his eyes, and it stoked the fire inside him as he saw her as lost as he was. He dug his fingers into the soft flesh of her thighs as he moved his mouth down her jaw. Her sweet sigh spurring him on. As he licked and lapped at the supple skin of her neck and shoulder, he got the unyielding urge to press his teeth against that perfect alabaster skin. He shook it off. Why would he want to mar such perfection?

And then a sharp streak of agonizing pain lanced through his body, making him pull away.

As another streak of pain licked through him, he backed away from her. She opened her eyes, hooded with lust. Her mouth pink and plump. Her skin glowing at him. She reached out for him, and he stepped towards her. But pain cascaded over his skin. He wanted to stop it. To go back to her welcoming embrace. Back to the bliss of her body.

But tonight was the full moon. And there was no stopping it.

Autumn hopped down from the counter, reaching for Torin. He looked like he was in excruciating pain. Had she done something wrong? His whole body tensed as he grit his teeth, closing his eyes against the agony. She wanted to stop whatever it was causing him so much pain, but...there was nothing she could do. She was helpless. Just like when her mother had gotten sick. Like when the evil men had stolen her away. Why was she always so goddamn helpless when people she cared about needed her?

Then, she heard it. The first bone cracking. Torin groaned as his shoulder popped out of its socket. The other one followed shortly after.

No, she thought, praying. *Please, not him. He can't be.*

But as she watched on in horror, she knew it was true. She backed away, her ass smashing into the counter again. She couldn't look away, praying each moment that she was imagining it. That she'd blink and Torin would be smiling down at her again.

In what seemed like no time, he stood before her. On four legs, whimpering as he tried to get his balance. His tail cracked into place, causing one last yelp. Then, he lifted his furry head, his ears drawn back to his head as he gazed at her. It was the one thing that wouldn't change. The eyes always remained the same. And he was no different than the rest, looking up at her with the same multi-colored eyes as always.

She shook her head at him, staring in disbelief. Not Torin. Not sweet, funny Torin. Her eyes darted over his new face. Tawny fur, long snout, wet nose. Not five minutes ago, she'd been kissing that face. The face of a monster.

With little warning, she turned away...and vomited in the sink. A moment later, fur slid under her palm as Torin nuzzled her hand. Jumping away, she snatched her hand away. She shook her head at him.

His head lowered as his ears fell back against his head again. Those hauntingly similar eyes widening.

How could you? she thought, her eyes swimming in tears. *How could you be one of them?*

He whimpered, looking at the floor. His eyes kept darting back to her though until he took a tentative step towards her.

She hurried back again, holding her hand up to stop him.

Lowering his gaze again, he gave her one last, sad look before turning and running from the room.

She could hear him clawing at the front door until she heard Lauren come and open it for him.

"What was he still doing in here, anyway?" Lauren thought aloud. Then she stepped into the kitchen and saw Autumn standing there shaking, those ugly blotches probably all over her face again. Damn tears. The kind woman's mouth frowned. "Now I know why he was still in here."

Autumn blushed through her tears, covering her blotchy face with her hands in shame. The more experienced woman probably knew exactly what Torin was doing in here. With her mouth. And throat. And... Autumn shivered at the memory, her shameful body flushing with heat. How could she still feel this way? Knowing what he was?!

"You seem torn, my dear," Lauren's soft voice interrupted her self-hatred.

Autumn nodded, trying to swipe the moisture from her face.

Lauren gave her a gentle smile, stepping over to her and pulling her into her softness.

Something inside her snapped at that moment. Some invisible dam breaking as the tears began anew, flooding onto Lauren's poor sweater in buckets. Lauren's arms tightened around her, which made her cry harder. How could this wonderful person be the mother of a monster? And how had she not seen any signs of his inner beast? She had always spotted them from miles away, but Torin had completely fooled her. With his smiling face, and witty words. Had it all been a mask to hide the monster within?

Lauren stood there with her while she cried through her confusion. Petting her hair and cooing at her. It brought all those memories of her mother back to her. Every small moment of content they'd had together in those early years of her life came flooding back.

"I know, dear," Lauren cooed. "It's such an adjustment. And I'm sure seeing Torin shift was a bit of a shock."

Autumn nodded into her shoulder. Shocked was the understatement of the century. She'd vomited for Zeus' sake.

"I'm surprised he ran away from you. He should have wanted to be attached to your hip right now."

Autumn lifted her head, scrunching her nose and shaking her head. No way. There would be no hip attachment to any fur of any kind. Period.

Lauren's big, brown eyes widened under her spectacles. "You...rejected him?"

Ummm...duh. Why would anyone want a monster around?

Lauren shook her head, her fingers touching her lips. "Oh, my. But, why, dear? I thought you liked him? Did he do something you didn't like?"

Autumn tilted her head, confused. There was no way to explain this non-verbally. She glanced around. Well, there weren't any men around, so maybe it was safe.

"He...he turned into a..." Gods, she couldn't even say it!

"A wolf?" Lauren asked.

"A monster," she whispered.

Lauren gasped. "Oh, dear gods, a monster?" She shook her head. "What did he do?"

Autumn gulped. "He touched me."

Lauren's eyes turned into saucers, her cheeks turning red as her brows furrowed. "Where did he touch you? If he did something unspeakable, I will tan his furry hide when he gets home, I swear to the gods!"

Taking a breath to steady her voice. "He put his..." Lauren's lip curled. "snout..." Gag. "On my hand."

Every ounce of fury melted away from Lauren's face. "Oh..." she paused, looking at her with confusion. "And that's it?"

Autumn shuttered and nodded. Wasn't that enough?!

"Well, dear. Lycans are very physical creatures. Even more so in wolf form. Without his ability to speak, Torin can really only communicate his emotions through touch." Sadness overwhelmed her face as she continued. "Although, I understand if that is a problem for you. Try to understand that it is part of his nature to crave physical touch. From you, in particular."

Autumn's stomach churned. Yes, she knew all about the lycan's...cravings. Jaxon and the others had come to her with them often during full moons. Gods, she was about to vomit again.

"Just stay in Torin's room and you'll be fine. I'll even join you once I find Kayline. The difficult child," Lauren muttered as she gave Autumn's hand a little pat and headed for the door.

Autumn was relieved to be alone again. It gave her stomach a chance to calm down. And her mind a chance to wrap around why Lauren hadn't seemed very phased by the whole "wolf touching" thing.

Back in Torin's bedroom, she huddled beneath his thick quilt as she stared into the fire. Her mind replaying the last eventful hour. She couldn't rationalize her behavior before Torin went all wolfy on her. She couldn't stand being touched by a man. It repulsed her. Always had. But for some incomprehensible reason, she wanted Torin's touch. Craved it with an intensity that mystified her. But why? What made Torin so...different?

Hours later, a high-pitched scream shattered the silence, driving Autumn from beneath the quilt as she bolted down the stairs towards the front door. It was unmistakably a woman's scream. A woman who needed help.

Outside, she blinked in the dim light. Only the moon, round and glowing, cast its eerie glow over the village. Lights flickered in a few windows of the houses, but it took Autumn a few seconds for her eyes to adjust.

A second scream sounded in the night and, this time, she recognized it. Lauren. Dear gods, what could make that woman scream like that? The woman who called men "cowards" and threatened them with war.

It was easy enough to follow the sound. And then she knew exactly what could make the strongest woman she knew scream in complete terror. Staring at the two of them from across the small clearing was a large, black wolf. One she knew all too well.

CHAPTER SIXTEEN

You're an idiot. Torin's four legs had carried him out into the woods. He had intended to take a long run far away from the village. And a certain redhead.

You knew from the beginning that it could never work. Torin growled under his breath as his paws pounded over the frozen ground. *After what she's gone through, she could never accept you.* But for some pathetic reason, he couldn't seem to get himself more than few hundred yards from the village edge. He was going in circles. Kind of like this dead-end relationship.

She thinks you're a monster.

Well, deep down he'd known she wouldn't like his furrier side. Which was why he'd tried to get her to stay in his room tonight.

But, no, the woman couldn't listen. Not to him, at least. Instead, she had to come moseying downstairs. Staring at him with those irresistible eyes. Kissing him with those equally irresistible lips. It was her own damn fault he'd shifted right in front of her. Because there was no way in Hades he would have been able to pull himself away from her before the shifting pains began.

A woman's screams tore through the chorus of howls drew his attention from his steamier thoughts. His keen ears picked up the pounding of human feet moving over the dead leaves and twigs of the forest. Sniffing the air, his chest constricted. He knew those scents. One he'd been familiar with since infanthood. The other had been permanently seared into his memory as the best smell of all time.

His paws pounded over the ground as he darted around trees and crashed through bushes in his race to reach them in time. Please, gods, let him reach them in time.

"Keep running," he heard his mother call. "Don't look back. Just run!"

She appeared suddenly as he dove through another thistle bush, her eyes widening as her mouth opened on a silent scream. Stumbling, she turned to run in another direction, and he spotted his mother not far behind her.

And the large black wolf trotting a few yards behind slowed to a halt as it spotted Torin. Torin raised his hackles and growled a warning. Which was ignored as the black wolf's dark eyes glinted with amusement.

"Torin, don't," his mother called from behind him.

He barked at her. *Get out of here!*

"He's twice your size," she continued. Why did no one ever listen to him?!

Keeping his gaze locked on the threat, he growled. Fuck his size. Sure he was on the smaller size, but size didn't matter. He'd proven at least that much over the years taking down others bigger than himself. Not quite as large as this bastard, but no matter. An enemy was an enemy no matter what their size.

"I'm going to find Talon. Stay here," his mother stern voice whispered just before he heard her creep away into the woods in the direction of the village.

As he and the other wolf began circling each other, he spotted Autumn hidden in a tree. Smart girl. She'd climbed up to where a wolf couldn't reach. Not until dawn at least. Because there was no shifting back until the full moon disappeared behind the distant mountains. Which, by the looks of it, wasn't too far off. He had to get this wild beast taken care of and quick.

Leaping, he aimed for the legs. The wolf raised up on his haunches, bringing his substantial weight down on Torin's head. Torin rolled from beneath him, clamping down on the meat of its front leg, drawing first blood.

The wolf growled, sinking its teeth into Torin's shoulder and yanking. Hard. Torin released the leg, bucking the larger wolf off him. The wolf almost got his face, but he jerked out of the way just in time, turning at the last moment to slash his claws into the wolf's side.

The wolf snarled at him; the amusement gone from its soulless, black eyes. It bounded forward, snapping at him. Torin's agility saved his ass (literally) a few times. He scratched the wolf's face up as it snapped at him, but it kept coming. When he tried to snap back at its jugular, it raised up on its haunches again. Torin went to rip the ugly mutt's throat out, but it slammed a paw into his face, forcing his snout down. And then Torin felt teeth sinking into the back of his neck, claws cutting open his ribs as the wolf went wild, whipping its head like a dog with a chew toy. And Torin was the chew toy.

Torin managed to shake him off but felt the warm oozing of blood down his backside. Not good. The wild animal went for his hindquarters, and Torin's injuries slowed him down, making it difficult to dart of the way. When Torin managed to clamp down on its snout, he put every ounce of strength he had into it. It yelped, yanking its snout free and leaving a few long, bloody gashes. Its eyes held murder as it crept back towards him. He should run for it. His one advantage was compromised. His speed and agility hindered by the amount of blood oozing from the wound across his shoulder, which screamed in agony with every step, every turn. His eyes darted to the trees where his mother and Autumn sat watching with horror-stricken faces.

But he couldn't do it. He refused to run like a coward, especially in front of her. He had to prove that he could protect her.

Torin let out a howl of pain as the wolf's jaw clamped down on the same wounded shoulder, hitting a tendon. Torin's leg gave out under the weight and pain as the crazy mutt had a field day with his shoulder.

Out of the corner of his eye, he spotted Autumn slowly climbing down the trunk, her tiny hands picking up a large branch and gripping it tight.

He barked at her, a strangled cry that revealed his weakened state. No, woman! Stay there. Ignoring the excruciating pain, he turned his head and sank his teeth into the wolf's side, pulling chunks of fur and skin from its body. Have to keep it distracted. Can't let it see her.

A loud bark sounded a few yards. and Torin tried to glimpse through the black fur to see where it was coming from. Was it another wolf? Which pack would it hail from? Because if it was another Blackmoon, he was done for.

Through the haze of pain and blackness, he spotted a third wolf crouched down on its front legs, snow white fur and icy blue eyes that glowed in the darkness. It barked at them. And through the air he caught its scent. It was female.

The black wolf must have caught it as well because it released Torin, lifting its head to lock onto the female. She raised up, her gaze firmly on the black wolf for a moment before taking off into the woods. The black wolf took off after her. Torin was all but forgotten as he struggled to stay conscious, limping towards the tree. But he managed to notice that the black wolf had a slight limp in its front leg as it chased after the female. Before he blacked out.

Autumn peeled herself from the tree, staring at the spot where Jaxon had disappeared. When he didn't come back after a few minutes, she registered a faint whimpering. A tawny wolf limped into the little glade. Claw marks littered its backside, and its face wore bloody teeth impressions.

Out of habit, Autumn retreated back into the bushes. Until she recognized the animal. His hazel eyes locked onto her just before he lost his strength to stand and crashed to the ground.

Rushing over, she knelt next to him, cringing at the sight of all the blood-stained snow. No one could lose all that and survive. His eyes fluttered, growing hazy.

Tears slid down her face as she forced herself to comb her fingers through his fur. Torin. He'd saved her from the monster. Again. And now, she would have to watch him die. Because she was a coward who hid in the bushes.

"Please, don't die," she croaked, but his eyes closed as his body shook violently. Her own body shook with sobs as she was forced to back away from him. But her tears slowed as she looked on in amazement, watching as he eventually came to lay naked and furless in the snow before her.

"Torin!"

His eyes popped open, darting around until they found her. She rushed back to him, slipping her palms over his cheeks.

"Torin, you're...you again."

He smiled up at her, still trying to charm her as he bled all over the snow. He opened his mouth, and she laugh-cried at him, knowing he'd be saying something to make her blush or roll her eyes at him. Maybe even both. But instead, his eyes rolled back in his head as it went limp beneath her hands.

Her smile vanished as she shook her head. "No," she groaned. "Please." Her fingers brushed the blood strands of hair from his face. "Say something." She speared her fingers through his hair, damp and sticky with blood. "C'mon, Torin. You always have something to say."

But he remained silent, unmoving. A sob tore from her as her chest squeezed the breath out of her. Her gaze darted over his body, cataloging his many wounds. Wounds she didn't know to heal. She had no special ability. She was human. Just a simple, useless human.

She lay her body down beside him, her tears slipping over his skin as she nestled into the crook of his neck.

"I smell him. He's over here."

"Blackmoon's men have gone back to into their territory," another male reported. "Son of a bitch, there's so much blood."

"Who's that with him?" the older voice asked.

"It's that girl, the red-haired one."

"Is she hurt?"

She lifted her head, seeing blurry faces in the dim light.

"She seems okay," the younger one answered.

The older one came into focus. "Get off him, girl," Talon snapped.

She furrowed her brows, clinging to Torin tighter.

The younger one squatted next to them. He looked familiar. Torin had introduced him, but she couldn't recall his name. Not that she cared right now. "Sweetheart, we need to get him to the healer. Please, step away."

She hesitated, reluctant to leave him for fear she'd never see him again.

"He's in good hands, I promise."

A healer, he'd said. Well, they were taking him to someone who had some skills. Because he wasn't getting any better with her help.

She took a breath and nodded, rising from the ground to watch the young man begin to hoist him over his shoulder.

Talon scowled at her before he took Torin from the younger one and took off running.

She glared at his back.

The young man whistled beside her, making her jump. "Talon does not like you, does he?"

She narrowed her eyes at him, thinking a moment and then shrugging.

He nodded. "Best not to care, anyway. Torin doesn't seem to."

Now, that was news. Why wouldn't Torin care what his own father thought of her. Family was...well, family, right?

"C'mon, sweetheart. I'll show you where our hard-ass Alpha is taking him. He'll want to see you when he wakes up, I'm sure."

She gave him a weak smile as tears welled in her eyes again, laying a hand on his arm in thanks.

He smiled back at her as he began to follow Talon's prints through the snow. "No need to thank me. Anyone who cares for my man, Torin, which you obviously do, is A-okay in my book."

She sniffled and nodded at him. He seemed okay in her book, too.

"I think he's waking up."

Torin didn't recognize the soft, lilting voice, but it permeated the thick fog of his mind.

"Yes, I believe so," his mother said. "I'll give you a few minutes with him before I call the healer in."

"Thank you," the beautiful voice responded, and his mother shuffled out the room.

Someone brushed his hair from his forehead. Soft and gentle. A whisper of a touch, but he felt it down to his toes. An all-too-familiar scent wafted over him, awakening his whole body.

"Autumn," he sighed, peeling his heavy lids open. "You're here."

A wave of relief swept through him as he saw her smiling down at him. She was safe. Jaxon hadn't gotten his filthy paws on her. And she was here. By his side. He'd thought his shifting might've scared her off for good.

She closed her eyes. "Yes, Torin. I'm here."

Oh, man. Hearing that gorgeous voice make music with his name made him want to thank her parents for the beautiful sound. He lifted his arm, finding his muscles groaning in protest. Laying his hand over her fingers that danced over his face, he smiled up at her. "I could listen to you talk forever."

Her cheeks flushed as she looked away. When she didn't respond, he pouted. "Oh, c'mon. Don't stop already," he teased.

She began to fidget, pulling her hand away.

Frowning, he tried to sit up and was greeted by a sharp pain in his ribs. "Did...did I say something wrong?"

Her brilliant green gaze finally met his again, but she didn't say anything.

"I won't know what I'm doing to upset you if you won't tell me," he coaxed. "And I don't want to upset you if I can help it."

He could tell she was mulling it over, and he tried to practice some patience. She deserved at least that much.

"The other men," she whispered, suddenly interested in the window. "They also...enjoyed my voice. The more I used it to beg and scream for them to stop, the more they wanted to continue."

Well, if that wasn't a hell of a good reason to stay silent all this time. That whole goddamn village had to be burned to the ground.

She slowly turned her head, forcing herself to look at him. "My voice has brought me nothing but misery."

His chest ached and he felt his eyes starting to sting. He had known she had suffered, the scar on her face making that obvious, but to hear it in her own voice made him want to hold her close and protect her from all the evil in this wretched world. And go downright medieval on those evil bastards that scarred her.

Scooping her hand up in his, he brought it to his mouth, placing a tender kiss on her knuckles. He gazed up at her, finding her struggling to breath. Although she didn't have that doe-eyed look of terror on her face.

"I am so sorry for what has happened to you," he murmured, hearing his voice crack through the tears he shed. "If you never want to speak again, I understand."

She stared at him for a long moment, tilting her head to the side. "Why are you crying?"

He sniffled and looked away, swiping at his damp face. "What they did to you...it's deplorable." Glancing back at her, he saw her eyes shimmering, haunted with the painful memories. "I'm sorry I wasn't there to save you."

Biting her lip as a tear slid down her rosy cheek, she took a deep breath. "No one could have saved me. My mother tried, but she was sick and weak. I don't even know when exactly she died. Nadene told me a few months after Jaxon bought me."

Out of instinct, he squeezed her hand. "Your mother was very brave and obviously loved you."

A few tears spilled onto her lap as she sniffled nodded her head. "Yes. I'm just...I'm not used to anyone caring about me. I haven't known what that feels like since I was four. And you...seem to care. But...you're one of them. A monster with a handsome face."

Being called a monster made him cringe. His own family (and pack, for that matter) had never viewed their shifting forms as anything other than a part of them. He could honestly say he'd feel lost without the ability. But he understood why she thought of him that way. Think positive.

"So, you think I'm handsome, huh?" he teased. Might as well try to lighten the mood.

Raising her eyebrow, she gave him a confused look. "Yes. I just said that. You are the only man I've ever actually enjoyed looking at."

The teasing smirk on his face faded away as he stared in disbelief. "Are you serious?"

She shrugged, still looking confused. "Why would I lie about that?"

Well, shit. That just lightened *his* mood up like the sun. He felt downright giddy about that little tidbit of information.

His mother peeked her head through the door, pushing her glasses back up the bridge of her nose. "Torin, dear, your father wants to speak with you for a few moments."

Autumn practically ran from the room. He glared at his father as he pushed through the door and stood at the foot of his bed.

'How are you feeling today, son?" he asked, crossing his arms over his chest.

Torin snickered. "Great. Considering I almost got eaten alive."

His father raised a brow. "It's your own fault. If you'd listened to me and gave the girl back, Bearpaw wouldn't have been in our territory in the first place."

He heard himself growl at his old man. "Get out," he snapped.

His father's gaze narrowed. "Do not take that tone of voice with me, boy."

Torin glared. "Fine. Get out, sir."

"Torin," his father growled back. After a long moment of angry glares, his father sighed. "No matter. Bearpaw won't be coming back again. I'll make sure of it."

"What are you planning on doing?" Because if they were attacking Blackmoon, he needed to heal faster and get in on that shit.

His father turned and walked toward the door. "I'm taking the girl back to Blackmoon. Myself. This has gone far enough. I'm not losing my only son because he can't accept the politics of how our world operates."

"What?!" Torin jumped from the bed, clasping his side as pain ripped through his ribs. "You can't do that!"

His father turned to give him a hard stare. "I am the Alpha of this pack. And I will not let you put all of us in jeopardy."

Limping towards his father, he yelled, "I will not let you take her back to that hellhole!"

Sadness flickered across his father's eyes for a moment before he hardened his face once more. "You will thank me for this one day, son," he muttered and walked out the door.

Torin tried to follow, but his legs wobbled, his body protesting his every step. He tore the door open. "No!" he screamed, catching his mother and Kay's attention in the hallway. His father's boots stomped down the hardwood at the other end of the long hallway. He couldn't let this happen. Autumn couldn't go back to Blackmoon. She'd suffered enough, and someone had to save her. He couldn't prevent all the damage Blackmoon had done before he'd met her, but now...there was only one way.

"I claim her!" he shouted, making all three members of his family snap their gazes towards him.

CHAPTER SEVENTEEN

His father looked furious. "What did you just say?"

Yeah, you heard me right, old man. He looked his father dead in the eye. "I claim her as my mate."

Boots clomping down the hallway, his father got in his face. "This is not something you do on a whim, son. Claiming a mate is a lifetime commitment. You can't just take it back once you get what you want."

Torin set his jaw, leaning into his father's face. "She is mine. And you can't take her from me."

"He's right, Talon." His mother stepped towards them, giving his father a nasty look. "Once he claims a mate, she is automatically protected by the pack."

"Stay out of this, Lauren!" his father snapped, making his mother's nostrils flare. His father ignored it, turning back towards him. "You can't claim her. I won't allow it."

"You can't do that!" Torin and his mother yelled in unison. "What the hell is your problem? Nessie can claim a fucking bloodsucker as a mate, but I can't claim Autumn?"

"Charlie didn't cause a war! Nessie had claimed him even before Blackmoon took him. Blackmoon stole him from us. They technically broke Pack Law, not us. But you committed a crime stealing that girl. She is their property."

"No," Torin snapped, getting right in his father's face. "She is mine. And as my mate, she isn't *property*. She is a member of this pack."

His father snarled at him before turning on his heel. Torin watched as his father stomped back down the hallway, determination and guilt bubbling in his clawed-up chest. He may have just saved Autumn, but he probably just sentenced his pack to war.

Autumn reached out and caught Torin as he tripped over another boulder. Despite Nikoli, the healer, warning him against this little trip, Torin had insisted on going for a hike. "You should be resting. Not gallivanting through the forest," Autumn said as she caught Torin stumbling over the large rocks.

Torin waved a hand. "I'll be fine. It's just a few scratches."

Autumn rolled her eyes. Stubborn man. He tripped over another boulder, and she reached for his arm to steady him. He pursed his lips as she helped him climb further up the hill. Not used to having a woman lend you a hand? Well, it was a novelty for her too. But a novelty she could get used to perhaps.

A few minutes later, he stopped and smiled over at her. "Okay. Almost there now. Close your eyes. It's a surprise."

She raised a brow at him, her lips tilting in response to his obvious excitement. "You're really a fan of surprises, aren't you?"

His grin widened. "Oh, you have no idea, gorgeous."

She huffed. "Would you stop calling me that? You know my name now."

He leaned over towards her, waggling his eyebrows. "That's gorgeous, too. Now, c'mon. Close those beautiful peepers."

Sighing, she complied. A zing of excitement creeping up her spine. Maybe she was a fan of surprises, too. Well, the Torin surprises, at least.

She felt his hand slide into hers as he pulled her forward.

"No peeking," he said, making her roll her eyes under her lids.

The incline of the hill steepened a bit, slowing their ascent. Eventually, though, Torin stopped and took a breath.

"You are gonna love this," he whispered, sending shivers over her skin that had nothing to do with the brisk breeze blowing against her face.

Raising her brows at him, she teased. "Really? You think you know me that well?" He certainly sounded confident.

He brushed his cheek over her ear. "Not as well as I'd like," he murmured against her skin.

Oh, the things that voice did to her. Even knowing what he was, he still got under her skin. Making her feel things she didn't always understand, but wanted more of nonetheless.

"Ready?"

"Yes," she breathed, the small caress not enough to quench the fire he'd stoked with one small stroke of his cheek.

"Okay. Open your eyes," he said, laying his chin on her shoulder as he wrapped her up in his arms.

Open my? Oh, right. Get your head out of the gutter, girl. That was certainly a first. Her? Thinking dirty? What was he doing to her?

She peeled her lids open, and all naughty thoughts melted away as she gaped at the scene before her.

On the edge of a cliff, she stood with Torin's body pressed against her back. The wind blowing through her wild hair as she took in all the beauty she never knew this world had to offer. In the valley below, two lakes nestled, patches of ice kissing the edges. The dark trees were dusted with white, and a mountain stood tall and proud in the distance, its snowy peaks meeting the bright, blue sky.

"Oh, my...it's amazing," she breathed. Her fingers curled as she ached for a brush.

She felt Torin smiling against her shoulder. "See, I told you you'd love it."

Still enraptured by the landscape, she simply nodded.

"I have another surprise for you, though," he chirped, moving away from her.

She managed to pull her gaze away as she turned to see what he was up to. "Do you give everyone this many surprises?"

Rummaging through the backpack he'd brought along, he shook his head. "Not usually."

"What makes me so special, then?"

His eyes snapped up to hers as his gaze roamed over her face. "Do you really want to know?"

Ummm, yes. She was dying to know why he treated her so differently than all the other men. What made him want to be so nice to her? Protect her? Give her presents?

"Well, I'll tell you after you're done," he said.

Done? Done what?

Out of his backpack came all of her painting supplies that he'd given her. She clapped her hands over her mouth, stifling an excited cry.

He gave her a big, goofy grin and got to work setting up her easel. When he was finished, he came over and grabbed her hand. "I hope I set it up right."

Her eyes shimmered as she stared at the easel set just in front of the breathtaking scene. Pulling her hand out of his, he looked back and gave her a confused look. She grasped the sides of that handsome face and gave him a big old smooch. A well-deserving one. "It's perfect," she whispered as she pulled away and gazed into his dazzled eyes.

Those smoochable lips curved into a sly smile. "And you wonder why I like surprising you so much..."

She blushed, scrunching her nose at his teasing. Rubbing her hands together, she gave the easel a little stroke. "Best get started then."

She really is amazingly talented, Torin thought as he sat on the blanket and watched the scene come to life with each stroke of Autumn's brush across the canvas. She captured each shadow of the distant mountains, every unique shade of green the forest below held, and even the plain white snow was made beautiful.

And with her attention on the canvas, he was able to ogle every inch of her at his leisure. The breeze rustled the stray strands of her wild, red hair that feel loose from the knot she'd tied on top of her head.

So engrossed in her work, she didn't seem to notice that her stomach was rumbling loud enough for even him to hear. Chuckling to himself, he got up and walked up behind her.

"How about you take a break to eat?" he asked, making her jerk. And causing a blotch of what was supposed to be bright blue sky smack across the mountain peak.

Pressing his lips together, he risked a peak at her face. She slowly turned her face to lay her angry gaze upon him.

"Ummmm...my bad," he muttered.

Nodding, she turned away from the painting. "Sneaking up on me is definitely your bad habit."

He gave her an apologetic grin and waved towards the blanket. "How about some delicious apple pie?"

She quirked a brow at him. "Pie? What is pie?"

He felt his jaw fall slack. "You've never had pie?"

Shrugging, she replied, "I don't think so. What's it taste like?"

"Well, you're gonna find out in a few seconds," he said, rushing over to the pack and pulling out the little containers he had packed. "Never had pie. It's a sacrilege," he muttered under his breath as he rooted out some utensils.

He caught her rolling her eyes as she sat down on the blanket. "Oh, you won't be rolling your eyes once you've tasted its deliciousness. Trust me."

She nodded, but her face was full of doubt. "I've never cared much about food, so..."

"That's because you've never had good food. Or, more importantly, *my* food, which is better than good. If I do say so myself."

"Mhm. We'll see," she murmured, taking the container he handed her.

"Wait! Wait!" he cried as he saw her going to pull the lid. "Now, this is your first time having my delectable creation. Savor it."

Sighing, she rolled her eyes again. "I'm about to throw your 'delectable creation' over the cliff and get back to my painting."

He paused, taken aback by her brashness. It was so...untimid of her. Like that kiss she'd shocked him with on the full moon.

He'd chalked it up to full moon craziness. Everyone went a little nuts around that time. But, no. As he gazed at her, her stare unflinching and her head cocked with attitude, he realized...she was full of fire. Fire she must've doused to survive in Blackmoon. And if that kiss was anything to go by...he was dying to feel the burn.

"Humor me," he teased. "Close your eyes."

"Again?" she huffed. "I already saw the pie."

Chuckling, he nodded. "I know. But I want you to smell it...ummm...properly."

Her head fell back in a dramatic show of exasperation.

"C'mon. Please. I made it just for you," he declared, giving her a big, fat grin.

Even though she sighed at him, he caught her lips curving into a smile. "Fine," she puffed, shaking her head as she closed her eyes.

He pecked her on the cheek. "Thank you, gorgeous."

Her eyes popped open, and her free hand came up to touch her cheek.

"Hey, now. Close your eyes."

She hesitated a moment before she finally shut her lids again.

Taking the container from her, he gently pulled the lid off. "Okay, now. Smell." He raised the container up to her face and watched as she took a deep breath, her mouth and eyes opening as she stared at the contents of the container.

"Oh, my," she breathed, her face leaning closer to the pie.

Nodding, he smirked. "Yeah. Smells good, huh?"

Her eyes rose, sparkling into his. "It smells amazing." He held a fork up and she nodded, reaching for it.

"Remember, savor it," he teased.

She nodded faster, and he handed the fork and pie over. She moaned, closing her eyes at the first bite. Letting her head fall back, she enjoyed the second bite with just as much enthusiasm.

"I take it you like it then?" he snickered.

"Mmmm, so good," she murmured with a full mouth.

Well, now that he had her in a good mood...

"So, just so you know. I don't make pie for just anyone."

She peeled her lids open. "Oh?"

He couldn't stop himself from fidgeting. "Yeah. I've only ever cooked for my family before."

Her fork stopped midway to her mouth as she stared at him. Lowering her hand, she tilted her head to the side. "What are you trying to say?

He took a breath and scooted closer to her, laying his hand on hers. "You're like family to me."

She stared at him for a long moment, and he saw her eyes start watering. "Really," she sniffled.

He nodded and smiled. "Yeah. Really. I couldn't imagine you not being here. And I'm going to make sure you can stay here as long as you want, no matter what."

Pie and fork were flung into the air together as her arms wrapped around his neck. "But why," she sobbed. "Why do you care so much? I'm nobody."

Pulling back, he cupped her face in his hands. "That's not true. You are just as much a somebody as anyone else is."

She shook her head and sniffled. "I don't even have a last name."

"Take mine, then," he whispered, stroking her cheek.

Her eyes widened as she stared into his. "Wh...what?"

"I told you that you're part of my family now."

"But...my being here is threatening your *real* family."

The truth of her words sank deep, making his heart cringe with guilt. But the thought of giving her up to Blackmoon made it feel like his heart would completely shatter. "Let me worry about that. You deserve a real family, too."

"You would risk your family for a nobody like me?"

"In Blackmoon, you may have been treated as a nobody. But here, with me...you are everything."

CHAPTER EIGHTEEN

Autumn threw her arms around him, wanting to cry and kiss him all at the same time. And then she realized she could. Because nothing was holding her back. Finally, after a lifetime, she was in complete control of her own destiny.

Staring into his eyes, she felt the familiar pull, dragging her body and heart closer to his. Maybe he could be part of her new destiny. The one she finally chose for herself.

And so, she kissed him, laying her lips on his for no other reason than simply because she wanted to. No hidden motive. No fear of the unknown. Just a woman kissing the man she wanted to kiss. And, oh, could this man kiss.

His clean, woodsy scent filled her lungs as he enveloped her within his embrace, slanting his mouth to capture hers perfectly. She felt every sweep of his tongue down to her toes. And, once again, he made her crave more. Of him. Of this. This moment. This feeling. She never thought she'd crave this kind of physical intimacy, but his kiss was more than she ever thought it could be. It wasn't a hot, sticky mess she had to bear. It was her heart racing with anticipation. Her fingers itching to sweep through his hair and clutch him tighter. Her mouth wanting another lifetime to taste him.

By the time they came up for a breath, they were both panting. And she was ready to dive back in for more. But, instead, he ran his mouth along the column of her throat drawing a deep sigh from her. Every new touch was a revelation, making her body shiver. Which had nothing to do with the cold and everything to do with this man's magic touch.

"Tell me if I'm going too fast," he murmured against her skin, drawing her out of her lustful haze for a moment.

"Too fast?" Her voice was little more than a tiny wisp of sound through the chilled air.

He pulled back to look into her eyes. "I don't want to do anything you don't want me to," he said, a serious note in his voice even as his eyes sparkled with lust. Literally. The gold flecks in his eyes must have caught the sunlight at the right angle to produce such a dazzling display. A girl could drown in eyes like that.

Correction. This girl *was* drowning in those eyes.

Her lips curved as she pulled him towards her. "I don't see how that's possible right now," she whispered, capturing his mouth again. When he took her bottom lip between his teeth, a zing of pleasure went through her. Gods, he was such a good kisser. She hoped she was half as good as he was. Because it's not like she ever cared before, or even cared to learn. Well, no time like the present...

She dove into the kiss with more enthusiasm, intent on learning every little move that made him clutch her a little tighter, groan a little louder, and dig his fingers into her hair.

"Gods, you're making me crazy," he whispered, his voice cracking with restrained lust.

"Is that a good thing?" she asked, not missing a step as she nipped his lip.

"It's a fucking great thing," he growled, tightening his grip on her hair as he yanked her body flush against his. And suddenly the obvious state of his arousal came into focus as his erection slammed against her hipbone. That's when she realized just exactly where they were headed if she allowed this kiss to continue. Because no man was ever content with just kissing. Hell, the way she was feeling, maybe she wasn't content with just kissing.

When his hand dove beneath her shirt, brushing across her stomach and making her skin tingle, she knew. Kissing would never be enough where this man was concerned. Already her body wept with want, flushed with heat despite the chilly air surrounding them. As if he had her wrapped in a warm bubble of desire that she never wanted to bust out of.

As she stood there, contemplating whether she should stop things while she still had the willpower, his free hand slid through her hair, tugging her head back so he could run a scorching trail of kisses over her collarbone. She wanted more of this. More of his hot mouth. More of his magic fingers. More of him.

She slid her fingers through his hair, holding him against her skin for just a moment longer before pulling his head up. His hooded gaze locked onto her face.

"What's wrong?" he asked, instantly stepping back from her. Giving her room to breathe. Too much room. She already missed his touch. "Did I go too fast?" She could see the worry in his gaze. What she didn't see was even an ounce of frustration. No huffing and puffing because she pushed him away. No flare of anger in his soft, hazel eyes. Just concern...for her.

That, more than even the incomprehensible desire she felt for the man, convinced her. He was the one. She felt it in even the deepest corners of her heart that she kept locked tight. Was wanting a man for such carnal pleasures normal? Well, she didn't know. But it felt good. It felt right.

"I don't know what I'm doing here, Torin. But," she whispered, stroking the sides of his face. "I---"

High-pitched screams tore through the calm air, making Autumn jump and clutch her chest. Torin's eyes got wide as he looked towards the dark forest behind them.

"Oh, gods. No."

"What is it? What's wrong?"

His chest heaved as he took great breaths of air, his brows furrowing and his mouth thinning with each breath. "I smell smoke." His eyes glowed bright gold as he gazed back at her. "A lot of it."

Torin saw Autumn's face fall at his words. She sucked in a breath as she pressed her tiny hand against her mouth. He turned to snatch up her paint supplies.

"Leave them," she snapped, her fingers gripping his own as she looked at him with wide eyes. "They're just things."

He gave her a stiff nod, wanting to hug her, but knowing there might not be time for that. Already he'd been gone too long.

"Go on ahead. I'll catch up."

His head whipped around to her. "Are you fucking insane? There's no way in hell I'm leaving you behind." Not alone. And not with Blackmoon prowling the woods unchecked as of late. And if his instincts were right about that smoke, they were prowling far too close to home at this very moment.

Her throat moved as she swallowed hard. "I'll just slow you down. There's no time, Torin."

Pulling her into his body, he gave her a stern look. "Didn't you hear a word I said?" When she gave him a bemused look, he continued. "You're my family, too. And I don't abandon family."

Her mouth fell open before she cupped his cheek, tears making her eyes glisten. "I don't deserve you," she murmured.

Smiling at her, he gave her a quick peck. "I think you got that backward, gorgeous. Now, I'll need to carry you if we want to get back to the village faster."

After she nodded, he scooped her up and began the long dash back to his home. He soon realized that sprinting was out of the question. Damn body of his had to heal faster.

The pit in Autumn's stomach gave a jolt as Whitemoon Village came into sight. Gasping, she scrambled out Torin's arms, allowing him to race ahead of her towards the billowing clouds of smoke and flame that poured out of the windows of several homes. The beautiful decorations in the village center were little more than piles of glittery ash. People scrambled from home to home carrying buckets of water and sopping wet quilts.

Amidst the chaos, she heard a dull pounding and looked up to find a small girl banging on an upstairs window. Heart jumping into her throat, she rushed towards the crowd of people. *Must save her.*

"There's a girl trapped upstairs!" she screamed at the nearest person she could find, her fear of speaking to tall, burly men overshadowed by her fear for the helpless little girl. The tall man followed her pointing finger, nodding as he caught sight of the girl and sprinted towards the door of the house. Autumn stood fidgeting, wishing she could do something to help, until the man reappeared in the doorway with the little girl in tow. He handed the coughing girl off to Autumn.

"Where's her mother?" Autumn asked.

The man only gave her a sad look and shook his head, making her heart sink for the poor child in her arms. She gulped and turned to find a familiar face. Someone she could ask to help the little girl more than she could. But as her eyes roamed over the scene before her, several familiar faces jumped out at her. And every one of them was unwelcome.

The faces of the men who'd caused her such misery dashed through the village, cackling as they snatched up little girls scurrying to get to their mothers. Dark images of her own past flitted through her mind. When she had been just as young. Only she had no mother to run to. Autumn clung the child in her arms whose mother had perished in the burning house behind them, determined not to let the child suffer the same fate she had. She took off, running to the only place she'd ever felt safe in her life. *They can't have her.*

As she dodged around more burning buildings, the screams and shouts echoing in her ears, she held back the tears of her guilty heart. She had caused this. Blackmoon had come for her. She looked down at the child in her arms. The motherless child. Her fault. It was all her fault.

When she got to her safe haven, it too was engulfed in flames. And then Torin walked through the smoke of his family home, cradling his mother's limp form in his arms.

CHAPTER NINETEEN

A sob tore from her chest as she looked at Lauren's face. A nasty burn covered her right cheek down to her collarbone.

"No, no, no," she muttered as her legs gave out and she crashed to the ground still cradling the child who wept in her arms.

"Miss Laurie?" the child cried, her innocent eyes widening as she caught sight of Lauren. "Miss Laurie? What's wrong with her?"

She and the child sobbed together as Torin knelt down, breathing into his mother's mouth.

"C'mon, Mum," he muttered between breaths. "Don't you dare die on me. Come back. Please."

Kay came sputtering out of the door, holding her arm over her face. "I'm going to murder those bastards from Black---Mum? Oh, my gods, Mum!" Kay crashed beside Torin, skimming her fingers over her mother's burned face. "No, Mum, no!"

Lauren gave a weak cough, followed by another and another, and a wave of sighs swept through them. More coughing and then Lauren sputtered out, "Save your sister."

"Kay's right here, Mum," Torin said, stroking his mother's hair as tears streamed down his cheeks.

"N..N...Ness---" Lauren's head lolled back, and she said no more.

"Mum! Mum!" Kay screamed.

Torin swept his hand down his mother's body. "She's still breathing. But those burns need to be treated before they get infected. I'll take her to the healer." His gaze finally landed on Autumn, taking in the fact that she held a child. "You should come, too."

"Tor...what about Nessie?"

"What about her?"

Kay gripped her brother's chin, forcing him to look at her. "They're trapped in the basement. It's still daylight."

Torin uttered every profanity he knew as the blackened walls and broken windows of Nikoli's house came into view. There would be no healing being performed in that ransack.

Kay stepped in front of him with that "I can't believe you" look in her eye. "Give me Mum. I'll try to find Nikoli---"

"I'm not leaving her." No way. Not happening.

And there went the hands on the hips. "Torin," Kay pressed. "They could be burning alive in that basement!"

"They're vampires. They'll be fine."

Kay clenched her fist as she rolled her eyes and huffed at him. "Vampires are vulnerable to fire."

Son of a bitch. She was right. Apparently, even super-special supernatural hybrids weren't invulnerable.

"I'll go find your father," Autumn chimed in, drawing his gaze from his stick-in-his-side sister. The tiny woman still carried the child in her arms, and he'd be lying if that sight wasn't having some kind of effect on him. But that little thought would have to wait for another time.

"My father?" he asked, wondering why on earth she'd volunteer to go find the one man in Whitemoon that might actually hand her over to the Blackmoon warriors plundering about.

Autumn's slender throat moved as she gulped and gave him a stiff nod. "The Alpha will be able to round up help the fastest, wouldn't he?"

Torin lifted his shoulder. "Well, yes, probably, but..."

"Then, I'll find him while you go save Nessie and Kay looks after your mother. I know you don't want to let her go, but Nessie needs you, and you know that Kay is capable of looking after your mother."

As she turned and walked away, Torin shook his head in amazement. Because he had seen the fear in her gaze and tremble in her body, and still she went towards the danger.

He carried his mother back towards their home, cringing at the sight of the rising flames. Kay ran off and returned with a few large, dripping blankets. Begrudgingly, he laid his mother in the driest patch he could find, and Kay threw the blankets at him. They landed in his face, and he glared at his sister for a moment before he threw them over his shoulders and dashed into the burning remnants of his childhood home.

Crumbling pieces of the ceiling pinged off the wet fabric as he ventured towards the basement. And every step he could hear the ominous creaking of weakening floorboards, threatening to collapse at any moment. But as he opened the door just enough to slide himself through and slam it shut again, he was relieved by the coolness that still radiated from his home's depths.

"Ness? Charlie?" he called, finding himself sending up a silent prayer that he didn't find them in a blackened crisp somewhere in the rubble.

The stairs creaked as he crept down the stairs, his eyes easily adjusting to the dim light and finding no one. He spent as much time as he could risk searching every dark corner, but he found nothing beyond a caved-in wall and a pile of dirt. They couldn't have been dumb enough to try to escape into the house, could they? Weren't vampires highly attuned to the rise and fall of the sun?

And then the roof above him disintegrated. Ash, smoke, and flames poured down on him and he realized he'd stayed too long.

Autumn darted through the village, trying to avoid every familiar Blackmoon face she came across, but it made tracking down Torin's father twice as difficult. She was taking too long. Lauren could already be fading away.

"Aren't you a pair of pretty ones?"

A chill ran up Autumn's spine as she turned to see one of those familiar faces giving her an ugly, crooked grin. Her mind raced as she contemplated her very few options. Her fight or flight instincts would kick in. Honestly, though, neither were viable options. Against a trained lycan warrior, what chance did she and the child really have? There was only one thing to do.

Setting the child on her feet, she crouched low and whispered, "Run as fast as you can until you find someone you know. Okay?"

Shaking like the little leaf she was, the child nodded and darted away. Autumn stood and set her shoulders back. "Leave the child and I'll go quietly."

The Blackmoon warrior seemed to mull it over for a few seconds as his gaze tracked back to the fleeing child. Ultimately, he chose the easier path. Typical. Snatching her arm, he nodded. "Very well."

As she was dragged away, she couldn't help but glance back at the only place she had ever experienced happiness. Or at least had the hope of happiness. Torin's face flashed through her mind. Lauren's and Kay's as well. Each step away from them chiseled another piece of her heart away, trapped in the tears that slid down her cheeks and fell to the ground. She had known them such a short time, but her heart would never forget them or their kindness.

At least the girl is safe, she thought as the burning village faded into the distance. Would the child know the horrors she'd been spared? Perhaps not. But Autumn knew, and that would have to be enough.

"What the hell are you doing down here?"

Coughing up ash and smoke, Torin peered through the haze. Nessie snatched up his hand and yanked him (a little too easily for his taste) towards the collapsed wall. "I came to get you and Charlie," he said. "Why the hell else would I be here?"

Nessie rolled her own hazel eyes at him and released his arm. "Where exactly did you plan on taking us?" She snapped the question at him as she clawed through the dirt. "In case you haven't noticed, the sun is still up, genius."

Torin clenched his fist, wondering why the fuck he had come down here. Didn't seem like she appreciated his concern much.

"Well," he ground out. "I wanted to make sure you weren't burned to a crisp. And I brought these." He held up the damp quilts in her face.

She eyed them before returning to her digging. "What are those supposed to do? We don't feel the cold. Vampires, remember?"

He glared down at her. "They were soaked in water to keep the flames off you both...genius."

She raised an eyebrow at him. "Oh. Well, then...thanks, I guess."

Gee, she was about as good at apologies as his father was. Well, she is his daughter. He threw the blankets next to the dirt pile. "Yeah, you're welcome."

It was her turn to glare now as he crouched down and began digging alongside her.

Another beam fell then, catching Nessie along her back. The splintered wood bounced off her sturdy frame, but she hissed as the flames licked through her shirt and seared her skin. He reached out to her (purely on instinct, of course). "Are you okay?"

"I'm fine," she snapped, refusing to look at him. "My back has endured much worse, trust me."

He pressed his lips together as a wave of sympathy swept through him. His mother had told him that his new sister had also suffered. In a different way, perhaps. But suffering was suffering. And like it or not, she was his family. In fact, had it not been for her and Charlie, he'd never have met Autumn. She'd still be trapped in Blackmoon. Still...suffering.

He laid a hand on Nessie's and that got her attention, her eyes snapping up to his. "Look. I know I haven't been exactly welcoming."

Nessie raised a brow as her lip quirked in a smirk. "Okay, let me stop you right there. Now is not the time for the mushy bullshit that I know neither of us wants to endure. So, how 'bout we just skip the touchy-feely and get out of this mess." She punched him in the shoulder and smiled. "You can thank me later, bro."

He gaped at her a moment longer as she returned to the dirt wall. "You're a piece of work, you know that."

A smile broke across her face as she made another dent in the wall, carving out a little cavern. "You aren't the first one to call me that. I doubt you'll be the last." She held out a hand as she stepped into the cavern.

"What's taking so long?" Charlie's head popped out of the dirt, making both of them jump. Nessie's head smashed into the roof of the cavern, and she turned to give Charlie an evil glare.

Another round of beams collapsed, but this time the whole roof of the basement came with it, smothering Torin. He coughed and lifted his arms, but a large chunk of the cement foundation came crashing down on his head. He heard both Nessie and Charlie curse before it was lights out and he heard no more.

CHAPTER TWENTY

Autumn slammed into the wall, feeling her arm bruise at the impact. Falling on her ass, she glared up at the man that had brought her back to this godforsaken shithole of a shed.

The man sneered down at her. "I'll make sure to let Jaxon know that his little whore is back and waiting for him."

When he stomped back out the door and she heard the faint click of a lock, she collapsed into a heap. There was no holding back the buckets of grief spilling from her eyes. Dark memories flashed through her mind, small bursts of light shining through as her memories of Torin, and his family flitted through in intervals. Those were the worst. Those made her cry out in agony as her glimpse of happiness faded into the darkness around her. Knowing what could have been made knowing what was about to happen even worse. Ten times worse. A thousand times worse.

Maybe she deserved this. She had brought death and destruction to the only ones who had ever shown her any kindness. And this was her punishment. Punishment for daring to dream of a life outside these four walls. Life without pain and misery. Oh, yes, she'd dreamed all right. Dreamed of a man with hazel eyes that sparkled in the sunlight. A man who had showed her what laughter was. What fun was. What...love was? Was that what this feeling was? As if without him, she'd surely drown in her sorrow.

Hours later, she had cried an ocean of tears. Until her eyes held no more, and her body shook with sheer exhaustion. And all she could do was wait. Wait to see who walked through that door. Would Torin come to her rescue a second time? Or would he finally realize that she wasn't worth the risk?

And then the lock clicked open.

Torin peeled his eyes open as he heard crashing around him.

"Torin? Nessie? Are you down here?" he heard his father's gruff voice calling.

"We're in here!" Nessie yelled from way too close making him clap his hands over his ears.

"Nessie? Is that you?"

Nessie huffed and, even in the darkness, he saw her crawling towards a wall of rocks, dirt, and broken pieces of what must have once been the basement ceiling. He became acutely aware of the pounding in his head, reminding him that said ceiling had fallen on him.

"What happened?" he asked, wondering why he wasn't lying beneath all that rubble.

Nessie whipped around, gasping. "Torin! You're okay!" He grunted as she threw herself on him and then just as quickly jumped off him. "I mean, ummm. I'm glad you're okay," she mumbled, her cheeks blushing. "You...uh...scared me for a minute there." She gave him a weak jab in the shoulder, which still made him wince.

Then, suddenly, a large chunk of the wall collapsed, allowing light to filter into their makeshift burrow. His father poked his head through the wall. "Are you two alright?"

They both nodded and Nessie helped him to his feet. Several more heads popped through the widening hole. Torin saw that most of the other Whitemoon Warriors were here to dig them out.

"Dude," Alaric called as Torin climbed through the hole and back into what remained of the basement. "I nearly shit myself when Kay told me you'd been dumb enough to come down here."

Nessie climbed out next and threw a glare towards his best friend. "Gee, thanks. Nice to know I'm so well liked around here."

Several of the other warriors groaned and mumbled rude comments. Torin shook his   head, "You guys are real assholes, you know that?"

That got a lot of them turning their heads. Even his father looked surprised.

"If it weren't for her, you'd have all found me buried under all that shit you just dug up. Probably dead. So, how about showing her some respect, you pricks."

There was an awkward silence as the others exchanged glances. Well, at least they were being silent assholes. For the moment.

"The sun set a few minutes ago," his father said.

Nessie gave an exasperated sigh. "Gods, we know. Vampire...well, part vampire, at least. We can sense when it sets."

His father looked taken aback, but simply nodded. "Um, right."

Okay, Nessie obviously hadn't warmed up to Talon as much as her mother had over the past few weeks. Of course, Eva, Nessie's mother, had loved the man twenty years ago. Torin had a sneaking suspicion Eva still did...and that his father might as well. The thought angered him, making him understand Nessie's hesitation. Even he had grown distant from his father since Eva and Nessie's arrival. And, honestly, he couldn't blame that on Nessie. She couldn't help who her biological father was or who her mother had loved (and might still). He really couldn't even blame that on Eva. She wasn't the married one, after all. In fact, he had to thank the two of them. If it weren't for them, he'd have never ventured into Blackmoon and found Autumn in the first place.

Speaking of Autumn...

"Pop," he called, catching his father's attention. "Is Autumn and the little girl okay now? Did you get them somewhere safe?"

Talon quirked a brow. "I haven't seen Autumn since the two of you left for that ridiculous picnic."

"What?!" Torin screamed

Dashing up the piles of debris onto the main floor of the house. He was distracted for only a moment by the sheer state of destruction his family home had been turned into. Black soot coated everything, and the dining room had been reduced to a giant hole into the basement. Ash and dust had settled on any furniture that remained, which wasn't much. But the loss of all that he owned did little to faze him. Houses could be rebuilt.

"Autumn?" he screamed as he bolted through the village, ignoring the pounding of his head and the ache in his body. "Autumn?!" His mind raced as he thought of the next place to look. But as each remaining house turned up empty and each face wasn't the one he wanted to see, his heart began to throb.

"She's gone," a tiny voice said when he stopped to catch his breath and try not to panic. He looked down to see the little girl that Autumn had held in her arms staring up at him with eyes shimmering with tears.

He knelt down and tried to smile at her, but his face wouldn't cooperate. "What do you mean?" he asked in as calm and soft a voice as he could manage.

The girl sniffled and pressed her lips together. "You're looking for the pretty red-haired lady, right?"

Torin nodded and swallowed a lump in his throat, hoping he'd heard her wrong the first time.

"She's gone," she whispered, bowing her head and wiping her runny nose with her dirty arm. "One of the bad men took her away." She lifted her head to stare at him again, a look more intense than he'd have expected from such a young child. "She went with them to save me."

Torin's breath caught in his throat as her words spilled over him. Rage, worry, and pride filled his chest. Those cruel bastards had his mate in their grimy claws...again. The tiny girl in front of him was here, safe, because of his mate's amazing selfishness. *And the woman thinks she doesn't deserve me.*

"Torin," his father's voice pulled him from his thoughts. He turned to face the man he'd looked up to his whole life, only to have his next words shatter all respect for the man. "You need to let her go."

Rising from his kneeling position, Torin gave his father a hard stare. "I don't fucking think so."

"They have recovered their stolen property. There will be no further reason for them..."

"You would allow that godforsaken pack to get away with what they have done?" Kayline screeched from behind him, her icy glare drilling into Talon. She stepped around him and got into the Alpha's face. "Your wife is fighting for her life because of those bastards!"

Talon's eyes widened. "What? Lauren?"

"Yeah. Lauren. The wife you've seemed to have forgotten the past few weeks, you selfish coward."

"How dare you speak to me like that!" Talon yelled. "Where is your mother?!"

"How dare you!" Kayline screamed back, pointing a finger up into Talon's face. "You act worried now! Now that Blackmoon has nearly killed her! And still you do nothing!"

The rage in his father's face melted away as he took a step away from Kayline, shaking his head. "I...I was just," he stuttered. "I didn't want a war. Over a slave."

"Do *not* blame Autumn for this," Torin growled, clenching his teeth.

Talon's eyes snapped up to his, narrowing. "I don't blame *her*."

Torin took a step forward. "You can blame me all you want. But, you know as well as I do that Blackmoon has been gunning for a reason for war since we invaded them to save Charlie."

"And you gave it to them!"

Guilt clawed at his insides as he stared into his father's eyes, as if staring into his own. He couldn't deny it. Rescuing Autumn *had* given Blackmoon the reason they'd needed. And the longer she'd stayed, the more he realized he couldn't let her go. Especially now. She was his mate, and he'd die before he let her go without a fight.

"Autumn is my mate. And the claim of a mate trumps the claim of a slave any day in the eyes of Pack Law." He knew it was true. Mates were treasured above all else in their world. To kill another's mate meant death if brought before the Leaders, a small group of the eldest and most powerful of the Alphas.

"You may have claimed her vocally, son. But until she bears the mark of a true mate, that claim holds no bearing on Pack Law. So, unless you're willing to force yourself on her..."

Torin growled again.

"Yeah, I didn't think so." Just then, Alaric and the other warriors hustled from the charred remains of their family home. "Any casualties?" his father asked.

"It's not looking good, sir," Alaric said as they circled around them. "It's looking like Blackmoon has straight-up kidnapped at least a dozen of our women and young girls. And we found Stefan and Lance both gutted just outside the village."

The three of them cursed loudly.

Torin was the first to speak as his father rubbed his forehead. "Autumn was one of them," he said, catching Alaric's gaze.

Alaric let out a long whistle and clapped Torin on the shoulder. "I'm sorry, brother. I know you liked her."

Liked her. Ha. That was the understatement of the year. "I've claimed her."

The other warriors all wore identical faces of shock at that news. "Dude," Alaric called.

"Yeah," Torin stated.

"What he's failing to mention is that he hasn't marked her yet," his father chimed in, glancing over at him with raised brows.

"Dude?" Alaric repeated, lifting his shoulder at him.

"Look," he said, holding a palm up. "Her life has been harder than any of you sissies can even imagine, so, no. I haven't pushed the sex button, yet, okay. But that doesn't matter. Blackmoon has taken more than just Autumn, which means..." He gave each warrior a hard gaze. "We're getting them back. Tonight."

Alaric's face broke into a wide grin. "Finally." He waggled his eyebrows at the others, who all chuckled and chimed in agreement.

His father grabbed his arm and yanked him to face him. "I did not call for an invasion," he growled.

"No," Torin agreed. "But you should have. It is our duty to protect our women and children."

"I'm going with you," Kayline said, her voice unwavering as Talon forgot about Torin and turned on her.

"The hell you are!" He went to snatch her arm, but she dashed away, disappearing down a dark alley in a moment. Talon took off after her, but, by the looks of it, he wasn't catching up anytime soon.

Alaric rubbed his hands together. "Let's get this party started."

CHAPTER TWENTY ONE

Autumn's body shook as the door creaked open. Was she doomed or saved?

"Ahhh." That one sound sent dread coursing through her already-shaking body. Well, now she knew her answer, at least. There was no more reason to hope for a better life.

"I knew you'd be back, baby cakes," Jaxon's booming voice echoed in the tiny room. "And from what Leroy tells me, you've even started using that voice of yours again." He pulled her up from the floor with one arm easily, grinning at her. "Let's see if we can get those pretty pipes singing, shall we?"

She contemplated whether she should try to fight back. Something inside her wanting to keep herself from being tainted worse than she already had been. Or maybe it was because now she knew what it felt like to actually want a man in that way. Whatever it was, the moment he touched her, she flailed. Her body rebelled against him, refusing to accept any more abuse from this wretched creature.

"Oh," he purred against her ear. "I should let you escape more often if this is how I'm rewarded when I get you back."

Although she thought she had no more tears left in her, her eyes proved her wrong. Because even though she knew she should stop the struggle - go limp in his arms and just let him get it over with - her heart just couldn't accept it now. Maybe, if she struggled enough, he'd accidentally kill her. Then, the misery of her existence would be over. What did she have left to live for now?

The door crashed open, and, damn her, her heart leapt as she snapped her head up. Praying for a miracle.

"Jaxon," the man who'd dragged her back here barked from the doorway. "They've come."

A smile broke across Jaxon's face. "Excellent." His weight lifted from her, letting her breathe a sigh of relief. "I'll be back later," he murmured to her, gripping her jaw and pressing a hard kiss on her.

After he'd dashed back out the door, she hopped to her feet and sprinted toward the one tiny window in the room. That brought the last time she'd been in this room rushing back to her. When she'd been slamming herself against the door trying to escape. Her eyes fell on the one exit from the room. What the hell, why not? She couldn't just sit here and do nothing. Not anymore.

Setting her shoulders back, she marched over to the door, pressing her ear against it. There were shouts far in the distance.

A quick check out the window confirmed that no one had stayed around to guard her. She shook the doorknob. Damn. But they had bothered to lock the door. Oh, well. Guess she'd be banging herself up again.

Slam. The door creaked, the little sound sparking some semblance of hope. Slam. That was a definite crack. Good gods, had they actually put the same broken door back on the hinges? Slam.

CRASH! The door cracked open, hanging from one hinge, and she stared at the opening. It worked. Holy gods, it had worked!

She almost jumped for joy, but no time for that nonsense. Sprinting out into the open, she veered left towards the forest. As she darted around one of the buildings on the village border...

Bang! Her body bounced off a very solid chest, making her stumble backwards. A hand shot out, gripping her arm and stopping her from falling.

"Autumn?"

Her head snapped up at the familiar voice. The most beautiful sounds she'd ever heard in her life. Followed by the most beautiful sight. "Torin!"

She jumped into Torin's arms, hearing his sweet gasp of surprise and the heavenly feel of his arms enveloping her in a feeling of complete safety. Cupping his face in her hands, she showered him in kisses. Because her heart was practically bursting at the seams. And then she remembered that Jaxon had literally just smashed his ugly face on hers.

Leaping away from him, she scrubbed her palm over her face. But she could still smell the monster all over her. Her clothes, her skin, even her hair. She needed to jump into a frozen lake!

"I'm sorry," she muttered. "I'm sorry. I know you can smell him on me. I'm sorry."

"The son of a bitch touched you?!" Fury flashed across his usually kind face, making her shrink back against the wall on instinct. But his anger melted away a moment later before he folded her inside his arms again. "You have nothing to be sorry for." He stepped back from her and took her hand in his. "Now, let's get you out of here."

Yes, please. She nodded and followed him, realizing she'd follow him just about anywhere.

They crept between buildings, making their way around the perimeter of the village. Until a violent roar echoed in the distance.

Torin froze at the sound, his eyes going wide. "Pop," he whispered. When a second roar joined the first, they both sucked in a breath. Because even Autumn recognized the second roar. "Oh, shit," Torin muttered, dashing toward the sound and dragging Autumn along with him.

"What is it?" Autumn asked as she struggled to keep up with Torin's pace.

Torin glanced back at her for only a moment. "It's a fucking Death Match."

Cursing himself to hell and back, Torin flew through the alleys, darting between buildings and eventually hoisting Autumn into his arms when her stamina ran out.

The other warriors soon came into sight, forming a circle around the two Alphas. He recognized his father instantly, the dusky brown fur and hazel eyes in sharp contrast to the pure black of Jaxon's coat and eyes. Black as the bastard's soul.

"What the fuck happened?" he asked as he joined the group of his own pack's warriors on one side of the circle. The real question was how the fuck did this happen? Because Torin knew what two Alphas in wolf form circling each other meant.

Alaric turned. "Their fucking Alpha challenged Talon to a Death Match. Can you believe that shit?"

Well...given Jaxon's reputation. Yeah. Sounds like something the arrogant son of a bitch would do.

"This isn't good," he muttered.

"Ya think," Alaric retorted.

Autumn tapped him on the shoulder, pulling his attention from the snarling and snapping happening in the ring. "I'm sorry. But what is a Death Match?"

"It's how power is exchanged in packs. Whoever kills the Alpha takes his place as head of the pack." Primitive and barbaric in nature, but many of their kind fit that description. It was no surprise their political system would be just as primitive and barbaric. Easily corrupted by power-hungry lunatics like Jaxon. Because becoming Alpha was a lifetime commitment. There was only one way out.

His father roared as Jaxon swiped a heavy claw along his side. Torin and the other warriors winced at the sight. A familiar voice cursed beside him.

He snapped his head around. "Kay! What the hell are you doing here? This is a battle, for gods' sakes."

Her icy eyes glowered at him, cold determination radiating from the depths. "It's my pack, too. I have just as much right to defend it as you do."

Looking over at Alaric, he narrowed his eyes. "Has she been here the whole time?"

Alaric shrugged. "She popped in not long after the fighting started. Probably to make sure your Pop was too distracted to notice."

He glanced back at his sister. The sneaky, stubborn woman that she was. But the fact that she remained standing (and from the looks of her barely even touched) spoke volumes.

Another roar echoed over the circle, drawing his attention back to the fight. A fight that would determine the fates of not just one, but two packs. It was a monumental moment.

Usually, a Death Match was an Alpha being challenged by another pack member looking to usurp their position. Two Alphas rarely battled. The Leaders highly discouraged it, probably because they didn't want one Alpha becoming more powerful than themselves. Apparently, Jaxon wasn't much concerned with the Leaders' preferences. Technically, he wasn't breaking any laws. Challenging another pack's Alpha was simply "frowned upon."

Talon's movements became unsteady. Blood oozed from several claw marks over his body. With Jaxon's black coat, it was hard to see if he had any injuries. But he seemed much steadier on his paws as he pounced on Talon's back, his jaws clamping down on the scruff of Talon's neck. After much struggling, his father managed to throw Jaxon off him.

The Blackmoon warriors shouted and cheered from their side of the circle. Jaxon darted towards Talon, making his father snap his jaws to nip Jaxon's nose, a hyper-sensitive part of a wolf's face. But Jaxon would dart away, circle around him before repeating the action again.

"The bastard is playing with him," Torin said.

"That's it. I'm going in there," Kay snapped, taking a step forward.

He snatched her arm, yanking her back to the outside of the circle. "Absolutely not. That Alpha would rip you apart without blinking."

Alaric grasped her other arm, holding her in place as she struggled. "You would only distract your father more, Kay."

Then, his father yelped as Jaxon tore a chunk from his throat, collapsing to the ground. The dusky brown wolf slowly shifted back to human form.

His wounds became even more apparent as the fur shrank away.   He was littered in deep gashes, oozing blood at an alarming rate.

"Pop!" Kay called, struggling against Alaric again.

Jaxon shifted back a moment later, sneering down at his victim.

Then, his father lifted his head, catching his gaze and reaching a shaking arm out to him. "Son," he called in a weak voice. "Please."

Torin's breath caught in his throat, knowing his father was dying. The man who'd raised him, taught him how to fight, how to defend himself against brutes like Blackmoon. Torin fought back the tears as he went to his father's side, crouching next to him.

"Pop," he croaked, his voice betraying him. Jaxon snickered behind them, knowing he'd won this match. Any moment, his father would die and the reign of power in Whitemoon would pass to him. Two packs. One Alpha. One crazy-ass motherfucking Alpha.

His father blinked up at him again. "Torin," he managed, blood beginning to gurgle up from his throat.

The tears he'd tried to conceal slid over his face as he laid a hand on his father's. "I'm so sorry, Pop."

As his father struggled to breathe through the blood, he gave a barely discernible nod.

Bellowing behind them, Jaxon turned to his comrades. "What a touching moment," he sneered, the other Blackmoon warriors laughing at their Alpha's sick joke. "Why don't you kiss your daddy goodbye?"

Torin closed his eyes, more tears coming before he lifted his head and locked onto Jaxon. In a flash of movement, he slammed his sword into his father's chest.

CHAPTER TWENTY THREE

utumn clapped her hands over her mouth as she watched Torin gut his own father. Why in the gods' names would he do that? She'd known they hadn't exactly been getting along, but she would've never expected this. They'd seemed like such a close family.

Jaxon's jaw dropped as he too realized what had just happened. He roared, leaping towards Torin, who drew his sword from his father's body and pointed it straight at the monster.

Staring down at the sword, Jaxon gave Torin a murderous glare. "You spoiled little brat," he growled. "Stealing my victory from under me."

What was he talking about? Torin had just murdered his own father. What victory was there in that?

Torin's jaw ticked. "With my father's dying breath, I am now the Alpha of Whitemoon. Challenge me if you wish, but you will lose. I am not so stupid to relinquish my weapon, and I will gut you before you finish shifting, you mutt."

Jaxon growled again, his eyes glowing with malice. "This means war," he said between clenched teeth.

"It's a little late for that," Torin snapped. "Take my father back to the village," he called without taking his eyes off Jaxon. Alaric and another warrior stepped up and lifted Talon. Once they were out of sight, Torin beckoned the rest of the warriors to his side. "Autumn," he called, holding his hand out.

Her gaze shifted from his hand to Jaxon's face. She couldn't help it. Her heart strained towards Torin, but fear kept her body in place. Torin called for her again, and she just couldn't bear the thought of going on without him. Even if Jaxon killed her for taking his hand, it would be worth it. He was worth the risk.

As she stared into Jaxon's narrowing gaze, she stepped forward and slid her fingers over Torin's palm. He gave her hand a squeeze. They moved forward as a group, forcing Jaxon and his men towards the tree line.

"Now!" Torin yelled, and they scattered just as arrows rained down on the enemy. Torin lifted her into his arms and bolted to the far edge of the forest. Roars rang through the night air as they ran further and further from the place that had stolen her innocence and her childhood. But as it shrank into the distance, the weight of her grief lifted, her heart swelling as she gazed up into her rescuer's face.

"Those archers were there the whole time, weren't they?"
Torin nodded.

"Why didn't your father call them?"

His throat moved, and he blinked rapidly. "My father..." his voice faltered before he cleared it. "My father believed in following Pack Law. Once Jaxon challenged him, Pack Law forbids the use of archers. The death blow has to be up close and personal, or it doesn't count."

Autumn sucked in a breath. "That's why you stabbed..."

"Yes," he whispered. "It was the only way to keep Jaxon from winning the match and taking over Whitemoon."

"Oh, Torin. You shouldn't have come back for me." Her lip trembled as she spoke. "Then none of this would have happened."

He paused for only a second, gazing down at her. "I never could have left you there. In that place. With him." He pressed his forehead against hers. "You mean too much to me."

As Whitemoon Village came into view, the dread that had pressed down on her dissipated. She was home. This was home. Gazing up at Torin, she felt her heart squeeze. *He* was home.

"Sir! Sir!" One of the other warriors came jogging towards them.

Torin set Autumn on her feet, but quickly captured her hand in his again. "Marcus, did you just call me 'sir'?"

Marcus raised a brow, lifting a shoulder. "Well, you are the new Alpha."

Torin pursed his lips and waved his hand through the air. "It's still Torin."

Marcus nodded. "Okay, boss." Torin growled at him. "Your mum's awake. Nik just told us when we got back."

Torin's fingers squeezed around hers. "Does she know about...Pop?"

Marcus pressed his lips together and shook his head.

Torin nodded. "Good. It's best I be the one to tell her." Turning, he looked at her, his eyes sad and weary. Lifting her hand up to his face, he gave it a gentle kiss. "Will you come with me?"

"Are...are you sure? Don't you just want family there to break the news to her?"

Torin's gaze intensified, boring into her very soul. "Yes, I do. Which is why I want you with me."

Oh, right. She had to get used to this family thing. Like the fact that she actually had one. She nodded. "Of course, I'll go with you."

"I want every warrior on patrol. Blackmoon isn't about to give us any peace anytime soon." Marcus gave a curt nod and took off.

Her heart raced faster with each step as they entered the healer's new house of practice. His old one had been reduced to little more than ash. She had no idea what to expect.

And when they finally entered Lauren's room, she had to press her lips together to keep from crying out. The one side of Lauren's face was covered in white gauze as well as her right hand. Several patches of her hair had been singed away. She and Kay both looked up as they entered the room.

Torin's grip on her hand tightened. "Mum." His voice cracked as he gazed at his mother's face.

Lauren's lips (or what they could see of them) curved in a crooked smile. "It's okay, dear. Don't blame yourself for this, which I know you're already doing."

Torin bowed his head and she spotted tears trickling down his nose. "I'm so sorry, Mum. I'm sorry I wasn't there to get you out sooner."

Lauren sighed and rolled her one good eye. "Torin, come here."

Torin did as she asked without hesitation.

Cupping her son's face in her hands, she gave him a stern look. "You saved my life. And that is what matters. This," she motioned to her own face. "Is not your doing. We all know who really did this. Hopefully, now, your father will see that Jaxon Bearpaw needs to be taken care of."

At the mention of his father, Autumn noticed Torin's body tense, and his eyes avert from his mother's face.

"Yeah, hopefully," Torin muttered.

Autumn frowned, her heart aching for this wonderful family that had taken such good care of her. Only now they were missing a piece. She swiped at her face, sniffing and clearing her throat. "Torin," she called. He turned his head to give her a grief-stricken look. "She needs to know."

Torin laid his hand atop his mother's. "Jaxon challenged Pop to a Death Match."

Lauren sucked in a breath, her eyes searching her son's face for answers. "Oh, gods. Your father...lost, didn't he? He's gone."

Torin nodded.

Lauren shook her head, her eye wide in a blank stare of shock and fear. "That means...Jaxon." She shuddered. "He's our new Alpha. Oh, gods. Oh, gods. We have to leave. Now."

Lauren went to move from the bed, but Torin placed a hand on her arm. "No, Mum. He's not the Alpha."

"What? Of course he is."

"No, he's not." Kayline's voice cracked from the doorway. Autumn had never seen her pale eyes so red, so full of sadness. It broke her heart seeing the spirited young woman look so...shattered.

Torin bowed his head, closing his eyes. "I had no choice." Glancing up, he caught his mother's shocked gaze. "I couldn't let him take over our pack."

Lauren nodded.

"I'm sorry, Mum," Torin croaked, his fingers tightening as he took a shaky breath. "Please don't hate me."

Lauren's shock melted away. Her one eye drooping and her mouth falling into a frown. Pulling her son into her body, she pet the back of his head.

Torin wept into his mother's shoulder, and she rocked him in that ancient maternal way. Watching the two of them brought tears to Autumn's eyes and an ache to her chest. Because she remembered. A vivid image of her own mother holding her in just the same way came flooding back. She recalled that feeling of love and tenderness. Of having that one person who would love you unconditionally. The woman who had haunted her dreams, her beautiful face always smeared with tears. It was her mother. On the day she couldn't save her. And somehow fate had given her the same face. The same wild red hair and pale, freckled skin. As if the universe was trying to make her remember. Or trying to make sure she'd never forget. Her mother had loved her. But hadn't been strong enough to save either of them.

And now fate had gifted her a second chance. Another person who cared for her. Someone she could care for. She sent up a silent thank you for being one of the lucky ones. Because she knew how lucky she was and how rare her circumstances were. So many like her didn't get rescued by a handsome stranger with a heart of gold. And with a family with hearts just as brilliant.

A few hours later, after checking in on the other warriors and setting up a quick guard schedule, he went to grab Autumn from his mother's room. They'd found an alternative home on the other side of the village. The dozen or so homes that remained standing were being used as temporary shelters while the village rebuilt itself. The months ahead would be the hardest the village faced since he'd been born. Homes to be rebuilt and refurnished, families grieving for the ones lost in this first battle. Because like it or not, his first true act as Alpha had been a declaration of war. The entire village had all been there when he'd broken the hard news. They had to know what was coming. It was the only way to be prepared. Alaric had looked a tad too happy about it, honestly. But Kayline had been pissed enough for everyone. Screaming and running off as was her signature move. Well, he'd deal with his emotional sister tomorrow. When she'd had time to cool off. Why were all the women in his family such hotheads? Well, except one.

As his bedroom door came into view, an odd sensation coursed through him. Grief weighed heavy on his heart, compounded by the guilt of his actions. He had saved his mate. At the expense of his father's life. And what made it worse? As he gazed over at Autumn walking beside him, he wasn't really sorry. He should be. His father had meant just as much to him as Autumn. How could he value one life more than another? But just as when he'd first laid eyes on her all those weeks ago, saving her had felt...right. Meant to be. As if fate had a hand in their chance encounter. And he'd run like hell chasing that fate. This fate. These last weeks had consisted of the best and worst moments of his life. But would he really trade all of his moments with Autumn to get his father back? Would he rather she be rotting in that shed while he and his father had another day to spar and joke about Kay's terrible cooking? As much as he hated to say it, no. He wouldn't. Saving this innocent woman had been the right thing to do. He had to believe that.

Walking into his room, he caught Autumn's hand with his own. He needed to tell her. She needed to know. And there was no point holding off the inevitable. He turned her to face him. "Will you sit with me for a minute?"

She gazed up at him, with those haunting eyes that seemed to reach inside his very soul, and nodded.

Leading her over to the bed, he sank down on the mattress beside her. "By now, I'm hoping you know how I feel about you."

Her lips curved into a tiny smile as she nodded.

"You seem pretty happy about that, which is good. It'll make what I'm about to say next easier for both of us."

Now, she quirked a brow. Yeah, he could bet she probably had no clue what he was talking about. Gods, did she even know about mates?

"Do you remember when I told you that you could have my last name?"

Those big, green eyes got bigger. "Torin..."

"I claimed you," he blurted out.

She blinked up at him. "What? You did what?"

"As my mate. I claimed you as my mate."

"Is...isn't that like...like marriage?"

"Kind of. Only we lycan won't ever divorce our mates. The mating ceremony bonds more than just bodies. We are soul bound." He stroked her cheek as he saw a twinge of fear in her eyes. "It's a vow of protection, of companionship, of...love."

Her eyes grew even bigger, if that was possible, shimmering at him. "Are you...saying...you love me?"

In one hell of a roundabout way. "Yes," he whispered, running his fingers over her face. "I love you."

She stared at him then. Unmoving, speechless, looking like she would burst into tears at any moment. But a few moments was all she needed. Her throat moved as she swallowed hard, her eyes searching his face. "I...I think I love you too."

He gave her a weak smile. "You think, huh?"

"I've never felt...this way...before."

"How do you feel?"

She hesitated for a moment. "Like...like without you, I'd fall apart. But with you, I've never felt stronger. Like every happy moment I'll ever have is in your eyes."

Okay, now he was about to burst into tears.

"Is that love?" she asked.

He shook his head, smiling like the fool he was for her. "I don't know, but whatever it is, I want that."

"Yeah?" Her face lit up in the most beautiful way.

He kissed her hand. "All I want is you."

She squeezed his hand, her eyes sparkling at him. "Show me."

"Show you?"

In a brazen act, she climbed atop him, straddling his hips. "I want to know what love feels like." She bent down, placing a scorching kiss on him, teasing at his mouth. "Show me, Torin. How does a man *love* his mate?"

She was taking this whole mate thing a hell of a lot better than he'd expected. Good gods, was this really happening? Her words were doing wicked things to his body. Already ready to show her *exactly* how *he* loved *her*.

But he pulled back, his fingers spearing through her wild tangles as he gazed at her. "Are you sure? We don't have to do this." Though, good gods, did he want to. "I understand how this might not be something you'd want to do."

She bit her lip as she stared at him. Not helping his body get the message. "I want to be with you."

Cupping her face, he smiled up at her. "You are with me. Like this. I will love you even if you don't want me...that way."

Her eyes shimmered at him as her fingers skimmed over his face, through his hair. "And *that* is exactly why I do want you...that way. Maybe I'm just being greedy. But I want *all* the love you can possibly give me."

Well, how could he possibly say no to that?

He pulled her down to him, skimming his lips across hers. Wanting her to feel even this gentle touch down to her toes. Like she'd die without one more touch from him. He kissed her slowly, gently, unhurried. Savoring every moment of her in his arms. And, oh, did she feel good. Like she was the something that had been missing from his arms. The puzzle piece that fit into his heart perfectly.

Her hands splayed on the warm skin beneath his shirt. The touch radiating through him, making him want to get closer. Feel more of her touch. Her scent drifted up to him, a sweet, heady perfume that drove him wild, feeding his starving senses. With his mate so close, her mouth on his, her hands on his body, it was hard not to completely devour her. Throw himself upon her and find himself inside her body. Bind them as true mates. One in body and soul.

Peeling his shirt off an inch at a time, she smiled up at him, a sexy glint in her eye. She enjoyed taking control. That was good. Because he enjoyed it, too. She could do whatever her precious heart wanted to him if she kept smiling at him like that.

"The first time I saw you like this," she purred, running her fingers down his chest, over the hard ridges of his abdomen. "My heart raced. I couldn't catch my breath. My fingers itched to touch you."

He kissed her hard and fast. "You take my breath away, gorgeous."

Scooping her into his arms, he carried her to the bed, setting her on her feet just beside it and climbing onto the mattress himself. He sprawled out, propping his head up on his hand. He patted the mattress next to him and wiggled his eyebrows at her.

She giggled at him before her eyes glazed over with lust, her fingers clutching the hem of her shirt. He watched with sweaty palms as she stripped out of each piece of clothing. Baring all that alabaster skin to his greedy gaze.

"I know you hate when I give you compliments, but I can't help myself. You are so beautiful."

She gave him a sheepish smile.

He shrugged his shoulder. "I know you're not the type to care about that stuff either."

Laying her hand on his face, she leaned in and pressed a gentle kiss on his lips. "I only care if you think I'm beautiful." She climbed in next to him, pressing herself against his body.

He captured her lips, deepening the kiss. Testing her limits as he skimmed his fingers over the deep curve of her waist. There was no resistance. No hesitation. She fell into his kiss with absolute trust.

He tried to take it slow. He really tried. But keeping his hands from venturing to all her secret places...well that wasn't happening. Because he wanted to know all of her body's secrets. He wanted to know that kissing her ear made her sigh, stroking her back made her arch into him, suckling her breasts made her pull him closer. It was knowledge he didn't just want, he needed. Pleasing his mate was priority number one.

"Gods, what are you doing to me?" she moaned as he ran his palm down the center of her abdomen, circling her belly button and smiling at her.

"I'm loving you like you asked," he whispered into her ear, stoking it with his tongue.

"But now I feel so...so...gods, I don't even have a word for it!"

His lips curved into a knowing smile. "I think I know what you need."

"What?"

He slipped his hand lower, keeping a watchful eye on her face. "You can tell me to stop at any time. Remember that. Okay?"

Her hooded eyes widened, but she nodded.

His fingertip slid over the little bud where he knew she required his attention. She sucked in a breath at the gentle touch. When he repeated the motion, her eyes fluttered. Again and again, he stroked her, watching her, amazed by how easily she succumbed to his touch. When she finally surrendered, shuddering as her body pulsed against his palm, instinct had him pushing her into the mattress, hovering over her, his shaft pressing against her, seeking her warmth.

His hand slid beneath her head, positioning it so he could look into her eyes as they became one. But she refused to look at him now.

CHAPTER TWENTY FOUR

Even though her body still shook with pleasure, cold dread coursed through her the moment she felt his maleness pressing against her. She knew she was safe here. With Torin. The man who loved her despite her contamination. She even knew he wouldn't hurt her, especially after the fireworks he'd just set off within her. But knowing all this didn't stop her body from freezing up. The love he'd just shown her had been a revelation to her, an experience she'd never thought to have, let alone enjoy. But there was no getting around the fact that he would still be shoving that thing inside her. Same as all the others.

And then the weight of his body lifted from her as he rolled to one side. The next moment she found herself scooped into his lap, his arms pulling her into an embrace.

"What are you doing?" This isn't what was supposed to come next. In fact, this (whatever this was) never came next.

He stroked her back as he gazed into her eyes. "I could tell something was wrong."

Her mouth fell open. "So you just...stopped? Just like that?"

He pressed his forehead against hers. "I told you I won't do anything you don't *want* me to."

"But...I *do* want you to."

He eyed her suspiciously. "Are you sure? You couldn't even look at me."

She gulped. Because he was right. "I'm sorry."

He cupped her face and gave her an intense look. "Gods, stop apologizing. You have nothing to be sorry about."

She cursed the tears that strayed from her eyes, sliding down her cheek. "I'm ruining this. I just wanted to feel...feel real love. And I can't even do that right." Gods, he deserved so much more than her.

"There is no right way."

She rolled her eyes. "Well, this isn't the right way. I know that much."

His lips curved in a little smirk. "We just have to find our way."

"What if I can't?"

"Then I'm gonna have a hell of a good time finding more ways to pleasure you."

"Really?"

"Gorgeous, I plan on watching you come for a very, very long time." He winked at her before he gently removed her from his lap and set her on the mattress. "In fact, let me start the fire I completely forgot about, and I'll show you."

And, good gods, did he ever show her. By the time he was through with her, her body was limp, exhaustion swiftly setting in. She fell asleep as soon as she felt Torin slide up her body, tucking her gently into his side.

She awoke hours later to the woodsy scent of her mate bringing her body back to life. Warm tingles coursed through her as she peeled her eyes open. She smiled as she spotted Torin's handsome face beside her. Drawn to the scent of him, wanting to feel the roughness of his stubbled chin, she leaned in, running her lips along his skin. It only took a few well-pleased kisses and he finally stirred.

He groaned, stretching his head to the side as she nuzzled the crook of his neck. "Someone woke up in a good mood," he murmured, wrapping his arms around her to tug her flush against him.

Nodding against his skin, she smiled. "Someone gave me a very good reason to."

His chest rumbled with a chortle before he pulled her up to take possession of her mouth.

Crash! The sound of the bedroom door banging open sent Autumn flying away from Torin. A tad too far as she swiftly landed on the floor scrambling to cover herself as she realized she was still naked.

"Tor." Alaric's familiar voice broke through the quiet morning air. "Shit, sorry," he mumbled as he threw his arm over his face.

"Learn to knock!" Torin snapped as he threw the comforter over her shaking body on the floor. He climbed down, kneeling next to her, naked and shameless. He glared over at Alaric, who snapped his head away and stared at the far wall.

"Marcus and Devon just reported in. Blackmoon has just crossed into our territory. They'll be here within the hour."

Torin cursed. "Gather the others. I'll meet you outside in five."

Alaric nodded and dashed from the room.

Torin looked into Autumn's wide eyes, a sense of sadness coming over him. His fingers grazed along her cheek. "I need to tell you something. And, this time, you may not like it."

Her already-frightful gaze widened further, but as much as he didn't want to tell her, she needed an explanation.

"You must stay hidden while I deal with Blackmoon. It is still day, so Nessie and Charlie will be forced to stay hidden as well. I will take you to them. Mum and Kay will be with you."

"Why?"

"Because until you bear the mark of a true mate, Blackmoon has right to take you from me."

"What mark?"

"It is a sort of tribal design that appears along a mate's skin once the bonding ritual is completed."

"I haven't seen these marks on any of the women..."

"The marks are only visible to the opposite sex. It's the human equivalent of the old wedding bands. The gods decided ours would be permanent. They only disappear if one's mate dies."

"And how do I get, umm, marked exactly?"

He hesitated a moment. "The bonding ritual must be performed."

She nodded, taking a step toward him. "Well, hurry up and do it, then."

"You would be bound to me forever."

"Right."

"Are you sure that's what you want? To be bound to...a man...forever?"

She gazed up at him, studying his face, a deep frown coming to her lips. "Are you sure this is what you want? I'm not exactly easy mate material. You could do loads better."

He took her little hands inside his own, kissing her fingers. "I have never been more sure of anything in my life."

Her frown flipped into a shy smile. Much better. "Well, then, what are you waiting for?"

He closed his eyes, pulling her into a tight embrace. "The ritual requires the joining of bodies, and...you're not ready for that." He cupped her face, sliding his thumbs over her lips as she tried to argue with him. "If and when you are, I will mark you quicker than you can say 'I love you.'" He paused a moment, running his lips across hers. "Well, maybe not that quickly."

He gave her a peck on her nose. "But for now, I need you safely tucked away with the rest of our family."

"Ours?"

"That's what being mates means. They're your family too now."

She threw her arms around him, giving a tight squeeze before dashing into her clothes.

He followed suit and they hurried down to Nessie and Charlie's new bunker. The cement floor had a large run thrown over it and there was nothing more than a bed in the room for now until they replaced all the furniture lost during the fires.

Nessie was pacing around the room, her hands opening and closing into fists. Charlie stood leaning against the wall, his gaze following his mate. Lauren sat on the bed, staring at the wall until the sound of their footsteps drew her attention. His mother took their hands. Gazing up at him with shimmering eyes, she croaked, "Stay away from Jaxon at all costs. He can't challenge you if he can't get to you."

"Mum..."

"I'm serious, Torin. I've lost too much to that bastard already."

He gave his Mum a hug, glancing up at Nessie's fierce face.

"I'll be up as soon as the sun sets."

"Nessie," Charlie growled.

She glared over at him. "Charlie," she growled back.

Torin sighed. "Please don't get any ideas from my bull-headed sister," he said to Autumn. "Hold up..." He glanced around the room. "Where's Kay?"

His mother sniffled. "I don't know. She ran off the moment she heard about Blackmoon coming."

He let out a long sigh. As if he didn't have enough on his plate. But he didn't have much time to track down his rebellious sister.

In fact, as Alaric's gruff yell echoed from the doorway upstairs, he knew he was out of time. Kay would have to wait. And he'd have to pray she found a good hidey-hole to ride out this battle.

"I have to go," he said, his eyes automatically turning to Autumn. She stepped forward, closing the distance between them and placing her hands on his face.

"You have to come back to me," she whispered. "I can't...I won't be able to...I need you."

He couldn't help the small smirk at the thought. If he made it back to her, he planned on taking an extended vacation enjoying every inch of her. "I plan on loving you a lifetime, gorgeous."

Pressing his lips against hers for just a moment, he relished the kiss before he forced himself to pull away and leave the bunker.

As soon as he was outside, he could hear the shouts of men just outside the village. The battle raged for hours, but they managed to drive them back. And Torin managed to steer clear of Jaxon.

But, alas, he couldn't avoid him forever it seemed. As much as he dodged between trees and other warriors, the clanking of metal on metal ringing in his ears as swords clashing and joining the chorus of battle around him, Jaxon caught up with him at last.

"I get the feeling you're avoiding me," Jaxon sneered as his sword smashed into his own.

Torin shrugged as he parried. "What can I say? Maniacal rapists aren't my type."

Jaxon's mouth curved as he swatted his sword away. "You won't be taking my victory away this time."

Growling, Torin slashed at him again. "Let's see if you fight like a man, or the monster I know you are."

An evil grin broke across Jaxon's face. "I fight...to win."

As the two parried each other, the force of the giant's blows radiated down his arm with every swing. Every clash shook his body, draining him bit by bit. But Torin had speed on his side. He flitted around the big brute in circles, managing to nick him a few times.

But none of the wounds were enough to weaken him. If anything, they seemed to spur the crazy bastard on. His swings came faster and harder. Torin could barely dodge them now.

Rolling out of the way, Torin came to crouch just in time to get a boot in the face, sending him flying. He landed hard, knocking the breath out of him. Jaxon's foot smashed down on his wrist, and his sword was swiftly kicked away.

Jaxon's sneering face looked down at him as he sprawled on the ground, his sword landing several yards away and well out of reach. "I am over a century older than you, boy. Violence is in my blood. I relish it. I bathe in it." He crouched down, tapping Torin on the cheek. "You didn't stand a chance."

He tried to roll away, yelping as Jaxon's sword sank into his shoulder, pinning him to the ground. A second glint of silver sparkled in the moonlight as Jaxon pulled a dagger from his boot.

This was it. He had let down his entire pack. His family. His mate. Everyone. This deranged monster was about to take over his pack.

"Stop!"

Suddenly, a familiar head of white-blonde hair stood over his body directly in front of Jaxon, straddling the sword wedge in Torin's shoulder.

"Kay, get out of here!" Torin growled, trying to push his sister off him. And here he'd thought he'd gotten lucky and she'd actually found a good hidey-hole to ride out the battle. But no, not Kay. Apparently, she wanted to be right in the action.

Jaxon's head lifted, the fingers still clutching the dagger gripping the hilt a tad tighter. His wide mouth curved in a smirk. "Well, aren't you a pretty pale thing. I'll deal with you in a second, princess."

"I offer myself as your mate in return for a vow of peace between our two packs."

Jaxon lowered his dagger, quirking a brow. "I am about to take control of two packs. What makes you think a woman would be worth more than that?"

Kay's throat moved as she swallowed hard, lifting her head to the sky, allowing the moonlight to illuminate her pale face.

And then he heard the distinct pop of her bones cracking.

Torin found himself shaking his head. Denial even though it was happening right before his eyes. Kay's skin shook, the bones beneath it moving, morphing. Fur erupted from her changing form.

"No," he whispered. "Kay..."

But, there she was. Standing on all fours with fur as white as snow, the same icy blue eyes shining out from her wolfish face.

He heard the dozens of men around him suck in harsh breaths at the spectacle. And the realization of what they'd just witnessed. A true lycana, untainted and pure.

"You!" Several voices called.

Torin turned, finding Charlie and Nessie staring at Kay's new form.

"It was you that warned us about..." Nessie's stunned gaze glanced over at Jaxon, narrowing. "Him."

Kay nodded her head and then shifted back a moment later. Making Torin snap his head away. He had no desire to see his sister naked.

But he caught Jaxon's face lighting up, a glint coming to his eyes as he smiled. "I accept your offer."

Jaxon took a step forward, but Kay stood her ground, throwing a stiff arm up. "Not so fast, buddy. I require a written agreement first."

"Kay, no!" Torin yelled, struggling against the sword still seated in his shoulder. He yanked it free and stumbled to his feet.

"And my friend happens to have one handy for us to sign," Kay continued, ignoring him. Again. Damn her!

He grabbed her arm, swinging her around, uncaring about her lack of clothes at the moment. "No!"

"I will not allow our pack to be put under his rule, Tor. Not while I can prevent it. You tried, brother. But Pack Law is on my side."

"She's right," Alaric said as he stepped out of the crowd, holding a piece of parchment. "As a pack lycana, she cannot be taken by a rival pack by force. Only her family, or herself, can offer her as a mate. She cannot be claimed without her consent. It is the Leader's Sacred Rule."

Torin clenched his teeth. Mates were coveted, but lycanas. They were prized, treasured. They were a pack's most valued asset. And they were to be protected above all else. For one simple fact. They had the highest chance of producing healthy lycan offspring. And the only ones that could produce more of their own kind.

"I do not agree to this," Torin snapped.

"But I do," Kay snapped back.

Alaric handed the parchment to Jaxon, who scanned over it. His mega-watt smile faded with each sentence. He lifted his gaze, looking over the parchment at Kay. "This...agreement...states that we must release all slaves in addition to a vow of peace, which by the way is to remain in effect as long as either of us lives."

Kay nodded. "You read that correctly."

Jaxon quirked a brow. "It also forbids me from touching you until after the next full moon during the bonding ritual."

Kay slammed her hands on her hips. "Do you want me or not?"

Jaxon's eyes flickered over her bare body, making Torin clench his fists. He stripped his shirt off, throwing it over Kay's shoulders and giving Jaxon a dirty look.

"Very well," Jaxon stated, scribbling a sloppy signature onto the parchment.

Alaric took the parchment form him and handed it to his sister.

With a shaking hand, Kay signed her own name.

CHAPTER TWENTY FIVE

The sound of Lauren's sobs tore a hole in Autumn's heart. She crossed the basement and took Kayline's hands in her own. Gulping down the lump in her throat, she shook her head at the young woman that already felt like a sister.

"I can't let you do this," she said, fighting to keep her voice from cracking. "I know...him. You cannot let him claim you like this. He will ruin you."

Kayline smiled, but it didn't reach her eyes. "I'm a big girl, and not nearly as innocent as you seem to think."

"No. No, Kay." Lauren sniffled, pulling Kayline into a tight embrace. "I won't let you go."

"I've already signed the contract."

"I don't care. Torin, tell her!"

Shaking, Autumn stepped towards the man she wanted more

than anything. But not like this. Not with his sister's happiness hanging over her. "This isn't right. I have to go back."

Torin shook his head, his jaw ticking. "It's too late for that now. Kay revealed herself. Her true self. Jaxon won't accept anything less than a lycana in exchange for a peace treaty."

"No!" Lauren's sobbing began again as she squeezed her daughter harder.

With a hesitant hand, Autumn tried to comfort the only two women to ever feel like family since the death of her mother. "We have to fix this," she murmured, turning to find Torin gone.

She turned back in time to catch a tear falling down Kayline's cheek as she closed her eyes, her lip quivering as she laid her head on her mother's shoulder.

Feeling her own eyes stinging with the threat of tears, Autumn fled the room. Her first instinct was to run to Torin's room, her safe place. Until she remembered that room and that entire house had been burned to the ground less than a week ago.

She found her way to Torin's new bedroom in this unfamiliar house. Her hand froze on the doorknob as a loud crash came from inside the room.

After taking a few deep breaths, she turned the knob and stepped into what used to be a sparsely furnished bedroom. Now, she stared wide-eyed at what was left of the furniture.

Across the room, Torin's forehead rested against the wall, his shoulders heaving through his own deep breaths. Autumn's heart clenched as the sheer weight of his despair hit her. Without speaking, she padded across the room and wrapped her arms around his waist. Laying her cheek against the strength of his back, they stood breathing together for long moments.

Before she could talk herself out of it, she opened her mouth and allowed those words that had soothed her once upon a time to wash over them.

Bright blue sky, deep blue sea
A world of endless beauty
I promise thee, in these dark times
You will know love, sweet child of mine
So shut your eyes and just let go
Dream away your worldly woes
One day, when you wake, my dear
All you seek will be revealed

Torin didn't move until her voice drifted into the silence. Then, he turned in her arms because she refused to let go of him. His red-brimmed eyes gazed down at her. His palm slid across her cheek, his thumb caressing her bottom lip as his mouth curved in a tiny smile. "The gods committed a crime letting a voice like that go silent for so long."

Her cheeks burned and she couldn't stop her gaze from falling away.

He slipped a finger beneath her chin, lifting her eyes to his again. "You're officially the most talented person I know."

She rolled her eyes at him, but there was no stopping the smile. He had an adorably aggravating talent for embarrassing her and making her feel worth his weight in gold at the same time.

"But your sister..."

His smile faltered and she immediately regretted saying anything. "I know."

"I can't stay here with you. Not like this."

"I told you. It's too late."

"I know what you said, but it feels wrong. It's like I'm trading getting my dream life for her nightmare. I'm not wor---"

His finger landed on her mouth, stopping her words. "You haven't been listening to me at all, have you?"

She tilted her head to the side and quirked a brow.

"The point is you're not in Blackmoon anymore. You're here.

And here, you're everything. You're worth anything."

She opened her mouth to argue with his ridiculousness, but his lips latched onto hers. His kiss took her voice, took all thoughts of leaving from her mind.

They sank to the floor in a tangle of passion that made her body heat, her fingers tingling in sweet anticipation. But that nagging feeling of guilt clawed its way through the lustful fog. She pulled her lips from his and held him at arm's length. "We have to stop."

The trail of kisses Torin was leaving on her neck stopped. He nodded and backed away. "Of course."

"We have to think of your sister."

His face fell as he looked away. "That's the last thing I wanted to think about in this moment."

"We have to save her."

Pulling them up from the floor, he huffed. "Don't you think I know that? She's my sister. I will find a way to save her if it kills me."

Autumn's eyes went wide. Because she knew without a doubt that he meant every word. He would die to save his sister.

She caressed his cheek. "I know you will. And I'll be here to help you. No matter what."

He smiled down at her, but she wanted nothing more than to take the pain in his eyes away. Raising on her tiptoes she pulled him into a kiss, the same way she had with that first kiss on the full moon. As he deepened the kiss, pulling her against him, she could feel his need for her with every measured squeeze of his hands, every timid sweep of his tongue. He wanted more, needed more, but she could feel him holding back. Not wanting to push her too far.

Her hands slipped under his shirt, relishing every ridge and groove of his hard body, the heat seeming to seep right into her bones. As her fingers grazed closer to his pants, she felt his muscles quiver beneath her touch. His grip tightened on her hips, pulling her closer. His erection pushed against her belly, but instead of frightening her, it set her body into a tidal wave of scorching need.

When she started pushing his leathers down over that delectable backside, he pulled back. He pushed her hands away, shaking his head. "You don't have to do this."

She nipped at his bottom lip. "I know. But I want to feel you." Her hands returned to her task of removing his leathers. "I want to watch your face as I ..." Her fingers wrapped around the hot length of him. He sucked in a breath, mouth open and almost irresistible. But as her palm slipped over his flesh and he let out a shaky breath, she couldn't miss out on the pleasure washing over his face.

As she explored the spots that made him tremble, the places that had his hips thrusting forward, she pushed the fear of the past back. Back to that deep, dark place in the back of her mind. That fear had no place in this moment. The thing sliding between her hands may have terrified her once, but she told herself they were not all the same. Torin had shown her that. Not all men were cruel. Not all men relished in the tortured cries of a woman in pain. Torin was different. His would be different.

When he let out a groan, the back of his head fell against the wall behind him. As she watched him, liquid heat pooled low in her belly.

As if he sensed her rising need, his hands snaked beneath her dress, slipping past her panties. Like before, there was no pain as his fingers pushed inside her. Instead, her made her body weep with want. She tried to concentrate on her own hand running over the length of him, but when he locked gazes with her, she realized she wanted more. She wanted all of him.

A streak of pleasure took her close to the edge. "I want you to mark me."

It took him a moment before his fingers paused. "What?"

She wriggled, groaning as his knuckle grazed across her clit and another zing brought her closer to release. "Mark me."

He tilted his head, his fingers moving inside her again. She panted, the pleasure building, climbing to almost unbearable levels.

"Please. I need you to mark me."

"You know what I have to do to mark you."

Her one hand cupped him, drawing a soft moan from him, as her other hand fisted in his hair. "Yes. Do it now. Before I change my mind."

He stared at her for long moments before a sexy smile spread across his face. He resumed his blissful assault on her body, making her groan his name, plead for relief. Just when she was about to reach her peak, he'd pull back just long enough to let him start again. She lost count how many times he brought her back down from the edge.

"Dammit, Torin!" Her frustration was getting the best of her. His fingers danced over her, building her up once more. She didn't know how much more she could take. Her whole body shook.

His hand wrapped around her waist, pulling her to straddle him. She heard her panties tearing and felt the tip of him press against her.

Don't look away. Don't look away. Watch him. Focus on him.

His mouth fell open on a shaky breath as he slid inside, but she stopped him midway.

She stared into his eyes. Those bright, beautiful eyes that sparkled every time he looked at her. That were dark with passion. Passion for her. She ran her palms up over his shoulders, cupping his face.

"I claim you, Torin Delaney."

The look of brief confusion on his face gave way to ecstasy as she sank onto him, taking him all in.

"You are mine," she growled, her fingers fisting in his hair again. She raised up until the tip of him almost slipped out of her before sinking down on him in one quick thrust. They groaned in unison. The deeper she took him, the higher she peaked. And when her legs felt like jelly, refusing to go on, Torin didn't miss a beat, flipping her beneath him and taking over in one swift movement.

He drove deeper, sliding against her every sensitive nerve, and she gasped in surprise at the raw pleasure his body was giving her. Pleasure she didn't know existed before this moment. His chest raised up and he slipped a hand between them, rubbing her until she finally shattered.

He cupped the back of her head, swallowing her screams as he thrust faster. Then, he lifted his head and pressed his forehead against hers.

"I claim you, Autumn Delaney. You are mine."

Her nails dug into his chest as she watched him fall over the edge and spill into her.

When he collapsed, rolling to one side to avoid crushing her, he tucked the matted tangles of her hair behind her ear and whispered, "I will love you long after those marks disappear."

She smiled and stroked his face. "There would be no love for me without you."

AUTHOR'S NOTE

Dear Reader,

Thank you so much for reading TEMPTED BY TWILIGHT. These two tugged at a few heartstrings as I wrote their story. And I'm looking forward to exploring this couple more in a future novella.

If you enjoyed reading, make sure to leave a review. Amazon and Goodreads are the most popular, but whichever platform you prefer is always appreciated. Here is a link to all the different stores for your convenience. Reviews are a huge help to indie authors like me.

Turn the page for an excerpt from Kayline's story, MARKED BY MOONLIGHT.

MARKED BY MOONLIGHT

CHAPTER ONE

*H*oly shit, what have I gotten myself into?

Hell, Kay. You have sent yourself to hell.

Well, couldn't argue with that giant slice of truth pie, could she? Kayline Delaney sat in her new room in the new house that would become her personal corner of hell. Hating the brown fur blanket she sat on that smelled of roadkill. And the wood-stained walls, dull and bare, making her feel like a caged animal.

That's because you are a caged animal. In a few hours, that crazy fuck of an Alpha will own you.

Even though she had volunteered for this mating, it didn't stop her body from shaking. Or her eyes from watering. Her blurry vision kept landing on her unpacked bag of personal belongings.

Other than a few changes of clothes, she hadn't pulled anything else from the bag. Nothing that would remind her of home. Or the family she had left behind. Her mother's scream as Torin gave her the news still echoed in her ears. Tears cascading down their cheeks as her mother tried to stop the monstrous asshole (whose actual name was Jaxon Bearpaw, but Kay preferred the name that suited him better) from dragging her away from the only home and the only people she had ever known.

And here she had remained for nearly three weeks. Unable to even take a proper piss without someone breathing down her neck. Gods, life sucked ass.

"Ah, here's my princess. Right where I left her."

Kay swiped at her face, squaring her shoulders before lifting her eyes up. Way up considering she was sitting and he was standing, and the man stood over seven feet. "Stop fucking calling me that, asshole."

His face broke into a wide grin as he crouched down in front of her. "I tell you what. You stop calling me 'asshole', and I'll stop calling you 'princess.'"

She narrowed her eyes on him, contemplating his proposal for a half a second before turning away from him and crossing her arms over her chest. "Forget it. I just decided I don't give a shit what you call me anyway."

Leroy coughed from the corner.

Jaxon smirked in front of her. "Yes, I agree, Leroy. Her sense of humor is very...refreshing. It will be fun having her around."

Leroy's face hardened at his brother's voice, and he simply nodded.

"Oh, yes, the fun we shall have, princess." Jaxon reached his hand forward, clenching his fist just inches from her face. She turned her head, not being able to stop the tiny smirk. Their eyes locked, his dark as his black soul to her blue and icy as her heart right now. She could see the stark frustration. Because the snarky bastard couldn't lay a finger on her without her explicit consent. Not until after the bonding ritual.

Which happens in a few hours, so wipe that fucking smirk off your face, stupid.

He dropped his hand, straightening his face and standing. "No matter. I came to give a gift to celebrate all the fun we're going to have."

Yep, smirk gone. She turned her head away again, looking at that damn wall she hated. Well, she liked it better than him so...

"I don't want it," she snapped.

His face was in front of her a millisecond later, but he was careful not to touch her. "I didn't ask if you wanted it," he growled. "I want to give it to you."

In his massive hand was a small box that he held in his open palm. She glared up at him. "I'm not taking it."

His nose scrunched as his lip curled. Opening the box himself, he lifted his gift out of it and presented it to her. It was a necklace, strands of dyed leather of different shades of blues, purples, and teals woven together beautifully. Her mind recognized its beauty, but she found it ugly and had every intention of tearing it to shreds when he left. Because she knew what this was. A symbol. He owned her and he wanted to make damn sure everyone knew it. Even though the prick would be undoubtedly marking her before moonset, setting permanent marks all over her body signaling to every other male that she was his. So, what the fuck did he need to give her this for?

Leroy sucked in breath from the corner, his own dark eyes narrowing on the necklace Jaxon held in his hand.

Kay quirked a brow and jerked her head toward him. "What's his problem?"

Jaxon closed his eyes and smiled. "My dear brother recognizes this. It belonged to our mother many, many years ago."

Leroy's nostrils flared as his fury blazed in his dark gaze. But a moment later, he snatched the door open and disappeared.

"Why would you give me your mother's necklace?"

Once again, his eyes met hers, an evil glare sparkling from their black depths. "I swore when my mother died that if I ever found another like her, I would make her mine."

Kay heard herself gasp, her fingers coming up to touch her lips. "Your...your mother was a---"

"Lycana, yes. I am very well acquainted with how...special,' he ground out. "Your kind is."

Gulping down a lump that had suddenly formed in her throat, she whispered. "That's why you agreed to the contract..."

He clenched his jaw as he straightened to his full height. "Don't play humble. You know just how special you are, and you used it to your full advantage when you presented that contract. You were betting on the fact that your...uniqueness would make you irresistible to me."

Heat rose in her cheeks as she dropped her gaze. Not like she could deny that. For all of Jaxon's countless and massive flaws, he had never lied to her. Well, not that she knew of. He'd never tried to pretend that love would ever be a part of this mating. Or that pain wouldn't be very much a part of it. No, he had been brutally honest about what to expect from him. If her sister-in-law, Autumn, hadn't convinced her exactly how bad it would be, Jaxon had filled in all the blanks. His sick idea of dirty talk, she supposed.

"Get out," she spat. "And take your fucking gift with you."

He smiled down at her, putting the necklace back in its box and pocketing it. "Until moonrise, princess."

Raul had had enough. For weeks now there had been an endless amount of lycans traveling far too close to his camp for comfort. Sure, he was in their territory, but he'd chosen this location because it nestled right on the border of two packs. Two packs that rarely traded or socialized. So, the area saw little activity because neither pack wanted to venture too close to the other pack's territory. Until recently, at least. Ever since that vampire and his human female had shown up a few weeks ago. He'd told them about the abandoned cabin and sent them on their way thinking that would be the last he'd see of them. Not even close.

They never spotted him, but he'd seen them (and a bunch of their new lycan friends) venture close to his camp again. He hadn't realized why until the familiar sounds of battle echoed through the trees hours later. After that, the two packs were constantly invading each other. One too many times now, they'd almost stumbled on his camp. And even though it seemed the other vampire had been accepted by one of the packs, there was no way he was betting on that kind of welcoming.

Raul shoved the last of his belongings into his oversized bag and threw it over his shoulder. He sighed to himself as he thought of the long journey and the endless hours of trekking through snow ahead of him. Luckily, being a vampire, he didn't feel the cold or the fact that he was long overdue for a new pair of boots.

A few hours and a pair of soaked feet later, his footsteps fell silent as he heard something rustling in the snow. His keen ears could pick up the clumsy footsteps of humans from miles away. But this one had snuck up on him. How? He could sense the human lurking somewhere in the distant trees. And he knew it was human because he had trained himself over the centuries to sense both vampire and lycan.

A moment later, flames whizzed past his head. He jerked, his eyes narrowing as he scanned the distance to locate the source. Flames once again appeared barely fifty feet from him, and his vision zoned in on the location just as those flames were hurled through the air. He dodged out of the way just in time.

With his speed, he got up close and personal with the...woman? Clearly human. Lycans had a distinct scent, which she didn't have. And he could hear her heart beating rapidly in her chest. So, not vampire, either.

Her hand reared back, probably preparing to hurl another fireball at him. He snatched it, pushing her back against the tree.

"You're human," he said. "How are you capa---?" Hissing, he released her arm as his palm seared painfully. Her arm from the elbow down glowed bright red.

"Wouldn't you like to know, vampire." She hurled another fireball at him, this time he was too close to dodge it completely, cringing as his shoulder got singed.

"Son of a ----." He stopped himself. No cursing in front of a lady.

When the bitch tries to roast me, I think cursing is perfectly acceptable.

He held his hands up. "I mean you no harm," he called, backing away from her.

That got him a nasty glare. "I've heard that before. And it's always been bullshit. And too bad for you I mean you lots of harm."

Well, that's just dandy. She's encountered vampires before. And it mustn't have ended well. Does that really surprise you? There's a reason you've been avoiding your own kind for the last century.

He cursed. Not holding it back this time as the bush behind him burst into flames, catching his pack on fire. He leapt forward, more curses flying from his mouth as a wave of fire came at him from the bush. He turned and ran, but not before noticing the woman's hands moving in unison with the flames. *Holy hell, she controls fire?! What the hell kind of human is that?!*

A wall of fire rose from the ground, blocking his escape. Fuck, this was bad. And pathetic. He turned and met the woman's eyes, purple eyes to be exact. Odd for a human.

Raising his arms, he called again. "I don't want to hurt you." Last chance, woman.

Her lips curved in a wicked smirk. "Don't want to? Or can't?"

Well, isn't she an arrogant one? He dropped his pack, kicking snow on it to douse the flames. He never dropped his gaze from her, though. "You have already called me 'vampire', girl. You know perfectly well that I can do worse than hurt you if I choose."

She quirked her brow at him. "As it stands. Your ass almost got lit on fire. My ass is still unscathed and perky as ever."

Touché. But that didn't mean he couldn't dish out some hurt of his own. If he wanted to. "You attacked me unprovoked."

She scoffed at him. "If I'd waited to be provoked to attack every vampire I've killed, I'd be the dead one."

Great. A fucking vampire hunter. Just his luck. Another ball of fire sailed his way and dodging them was becoming problematic given every which way he turned seemed to be engulfed in flames.

She took a step closer, her lips still curved in a sly smile. "Getting a little toasty for your cold heart?"

Clenching his jaw, he gave her a hard look. His skin tightened, which was another bad sign for him. Dawn was closing in. And he couldn't be stuck out in the open with crazy fire lady here. "Last warning. Leave me pass."

Her smile widened. "Now, why would I do that when I have you right where I want you?" More flames licked too close to him.

"Have it your way then," he muttered, grabbing a branch from the ground and racing toward her. As he raised it above his head, it exploded, ash falling into his eyes.

"How gentlemanly of you letting me have my way." And then he heard himself scream as searing pain licked over his face.

MARKED BY

MOONLIGHT

released (or will release) in May 2022

Please visit www.nicholewolfe.com for information on how to
order your copy

NEWSLETTER SIGNUP

Would you like to read Charlie and Nessie's story for free? If so, sign up for my <u>newsletter</u> to get the full-length Forbidden Fates prequel novel, BITTEN BY DARKNESS.

If you're already signed up for my newsletter, thank you! I hope you enjoy your free e-book and stay tuned for more updates, discounts, and exclusive giveaways.

ABOUT THE AUTHOR

NICHOLE WOLFE lives in a small village in Pennsylvania with her high school sweetheart, their two children, and two furbabies. When not working on her endless author to-do list, she can be found cooking for her family, gardening, eating at her favorite Italian restaurant, and haunting her local Dunkin Donuts. Find out more at her website.

9 781737 274926